HERE'S WHAT OTHERS
ARE SAYING ABOUT
KEITH A. ROBINSON'S
ORIGINS TRILOGY:

Logic's End is a great read, and I highly recommend it. It explores the question of what life would be like on a planet where evolution really did happen. The surprising result helps the reader to see why life on Earth must be the result of special creation. For those interested in science fiction but who are tired of all the evolutionary nonsense, *Logic's End* is a refreshing alternative.

—Jason Lisle, PhD, Astrophysicist
Institute for Creation Research

In this book, Robinson has discovered a 'novel' way to communicate vital information to young adults and readers of all ages. Mainstream indoctrination on the origin of species and the age of the earth are regularly encountered and have long needed combating. Through this unique story, truth is conveyed.

—Dr. John D. Morris President
Institute for Creation Research

Pyramid of the Ancients will challenge you to reconsider the conventional wisdom concerning the history of our world.

—Tim Chaffey, Writer/Speaker
Answers in Genesis, Co-author of
Old-Earth Creationism on Trial

Escaping the Cataclysm is an edge-of-your-seat thrill ride back through time. It brilliantly explains the plausibility of the biblical account of history, especially Noah's Flood. It also explores details of the feasibility of the Ark itself and the Flood's impact on the earth. A great read!

—Julie Cave
Author of *The Dinah Harris Mysteries series*

Picking up where *Pyramid of the Ancients* leaves off, *Escaping the Cataclysm* hits the ground with both feet running. I found my faith renewed again and again as I was reminded of the many arguments that demonstrate why evolution cannot be the explanation for our origins.

—Joe Westbrook
Co-author of *The Truth Chronicles*

BAB AL-JIHAD

Joshua,

Gal 1: 8 - 9

Keith A.

Robinson

BAB AL-JIHAD

THE TARTARUS CHRONICLES BOOK 3

KEITH A. ROBINSON

Cover design by Jas Tham and Melody Christian
Interior design by Melody Christian

Published in the United States of America ISBN: 978-1544035062
1. Fiction / Christian / General
2. Fiction / Dystopian

OTHER NOVELS BY KEITH A. ROBINSON

THE ORIGINS TRILOGY

Book 1: *Logic's End*
Book 2: *Pyramid of the Ancients*
Book 3: *Escaping the Cataclysm*

THE TARTARUS CHRONICLES

Book 1: *Elysium*
Book 2: *Dehali*
Book 3: *Bab al-Jihad*
Book 4: *Labyrinth*

To my readers –
It is always a humbling experience to hear how my books are making a difference in your lives. Your excitement and interest in my work is what keeps me writing. Please send more feedback!

ACKNOWLEDGMENTS

To Jas Tham, my cover artist. It has been a pleasure working with you for the past couple of years. I thank God that he connected us. Your work always amazes me.

To my graphic artist, Melody Christian. Thank you for making my work looks its best.

To my wife, Stephanie. You are the perfect helpmate. I could never ask for a greater, more supportive partner. I can't believe God gave me a wife that actually likes science fiction!

To my children. As always, I pray this book will be a lasting testimony to you about what your father believes. The journal entries from Steven are particularly heartfelt.

To my Lord and King. Father, use these words to bring eternal souls into a closer walk with you.

CONTENTS

1

RUMORS AND WARNINGS

Beams of piercing white shredded the nearly complete darkness, sending rays of purplish light bouncing in every direction as they reflected off the nearby, violet-hued cavern walls. The intruding beams emanated from several large bulbs mounted on the front and top of a large vehicle that sped rapidly through the thirty-foot-wide tunnel. The rocks and protruding vegetation proved to be no deterrent to the vehicle as it floated smoothly along on jets of blue, completely oblivious to the rough terrain below.

"How much farther? I've gotta go to the bathroom!"

The driver, unamused by the comment, turned to look at the man sitting in the passenger seat. "Shut up, Xavier. I'm not in the mood for your witless banter. You know where the nav map is. Figure it out yourself!"

Xavier leaned back in his seat and ran a hand through his wavy, black hair. Turning to look at the Arabian man who was currently driving the Spelunker, he frowned. "Lighten up, boss. You've been more moody than a *Pandora's Box* addict whose session just ended ever since we left Dehali. Even for someone with an exceptional gift of charm and wit such as myself, your sour mood has started taxing my patience after three and a half straight days of sitting in the same vehicle. Look, even Charon's normally bright and bubbly demeanor has been affected by your toxic vibes. Right, Charon?"

The only response Xavier received from the burly mercenary sitting behind him was a string of mumbled curses and a punch against the back of his seat. "See, Raptor?" Xavier continued with a look of feigned seriousness. "Now you've got Charon spouting profanities! And you know how much church boy in the backseat hates it when we swear."

This latest jest finally succeeded in penetrating Raptor's dark musings, causing a slight grin to creep its way onto his face. "And we definitely wouldn't want to upset him," Raptor mumbled under his breath as he glanced at the display on his dashboard that showed an image of the four passengers in the rear of the vehicle. To his mild disappointment, Braedon, who sat next to Kianna in the far back, seemed completely unfazed by the verbal jabs. In fact, judging by the blank stare on his face as he gazed out the window, Raptor guessed that the entire conversation went completely unnoticed by the Christian man.

"Well, for those of us who *can't* easily see the nav map, would you mind giving us an update? If not, then take your 'exceptional charm and wit' out of the front seat so someone who is actually helpful can take over," Jade said snidely toward Xavier from where she sat behind the driver's seat. An irritated chirp came from the gray, squirrel-like pet *mindim* that was perched on her shoulder, almost as if the small mammal was punctuating her master's last statement.

"Hey," Xavier said defensively, throwing a hurt look toward the Chinese woman. "No need to get hostile. Just give me a sec—"

"We're about five minutes from our stop," Raptor interrupted. "When we get there, I need all of you to stay in the Spelunker," he said, raising his voice slightly to make sure everyone heard his instructions. "The people in these Fringe villages don't have much love for foreigners. It shouldn't take me long to get what we need. This is the last stop before we reach the city."

As promised, within five minutes the tunnel began to widen to more than two hundred feet across. Lamps hanging from the walls and ceiling lit up the tunnel and illuminated a row of buildings that lined the left wall. Ahead, a gap between the buildings revealed a second tunnel with a sign posted above it indicating that it led toward another village on the outskirts of the city of Bab al-Jihad.

Disengaging the computerized driver, Raptor brought the hovervan to a stop in front of one of the larger stores, opened his door, and climbed out of the idling vehicle. Closing the door without a word, he headed inside the nearest shop.

After only twenty-five minutes of waiting, Xavier sat up in his chair as Raptor exited a building and headed back toward the Spelunker, his arms filled with several packages. A moment later, Xavier keyed the driver's door open. Making sure that there were no other pedestrians nearby, Raptor passed the parcels to Xavier, then climbed inside the Spelunker.

"Any problems?" Charon asked once Raptor had closed the door.

"None. However, the people here are very edgy."

"Edgy, as in 'expecting a war to break out' edgy or, 'there might be an earthquake at any time' edgy?" Jade asked.

"Both, I think," Raptor replied. Touching the panel on the dashboard, he engaged the computer driver, sending the vehicle moving down the tunnel once more. "I overheard a couple of hushed conversations about each possibility. Also, several people were buying survival supplies like flashlights, canned foods, personal generators, et cetera. The population knows that, one way or another, things are heating up."

"All the more reason for us to get this finished and get out of the area," Charon stated. "I still think—"

"Yes, Charon, we know what you think," Raptor snapped, his own stress causing him to lash out at his best friend. "You've made it perfectly clear numerous times that you think we should forget all about rescuing Gunther and Travis!"

"And I'll continue to say it!" Charon snapped back. "Until you see what kind of idiotic choice you're making! This isn't our war!"

"Nobody's got a blaster to your head forcing you to come with us! If you want out, just say so, and you can leave right now! But if you choose to stay, then this is the *last time* I want to hear your 'opinion'!"

Charon glared at his friend for several tense seconds, the expression on his face leaving the others to wonder if he was seriously considering taking Raptor up on his offer. At last he responded. "Fine. Have it your way." Leaning back in his seat, Charon turned to look out the window, putting an end to the confrontation.

"Oooookaaay then," Xavier said hesitantly. "I'm glad we got that out of the way."

Jade cast a quick glance toward Charon to make sure it really *was* "out of the way," then leaned forward. "So, what's our next move?"

Grabbing the steering wheel, Raptor switched off the computer and took control of the vehicle without responding to the question. The autopilot had taken them out of the village and back into the tunnel that led toward the city. However, Raptor found a smaller opening on the right and brought the hovervan to a stop inside a secluded cavern. Several feet in front of the Spelunker was a steep slope that led down to a rocky ravine fifty feet long and only half that wide. Shutting off the engine, he turned in his seat to address the entire group.

"You two in the back, listen up," he called out toward Brae-don and Kianna. "We're about twenty minutes away from the city. Before we get there, I need all of you to understand what we're about to get ourselves into.

"As most of you know already, the city of Bab al-Jihad is the center of Islamic belief and ideology in Tartarus. It is under the rule of the Islamic state known as the Ahmed Caliphate, after the current Imam Rasul Karim Ahmed. His military branch is called the Army of the Ahmed Caliphate, or AAC for short."

"Whoa, hold on a minute," Xavier interjected. "Speak English, please. Am I the only one who's confused by what he just said?"

Irritated, Raptor fought to maintain his composure. "Look, I don't have time to go into details. Rasul Ahmed is both a type of priest, or imam, as well as a political and religious leader who is seen as a successor to the prophet Muhammad and Allah's representative. That leader is called a *khalifah*, or caliph. His rule is called a caliphate. Got it? Good. Now, may I continue, please?" Raptor finished with a sarcastic look toward Xavier.

"Unfortunately for the rest of Tartarus, the Ahmed Caliphate subscribes to the radical interpretation of the Qur'an, or Koran —the Islamic holy book," Raptor continued, his last bit of explanation accompanied by an impatient glare thrown in Xavier's direction. "He believes strongly in the verses that talk about fighting against infidels in a holy war."

"Jihad," Braedon said. Since he had been almost completely silent for the past several days, his comment caused the others to turn toward him in surprise.

"Yes, and no," Raptor said. "The best interpretation of the word 'jihad' is simply 'struggle' or 'resisting' and it mostly refers to the inner struggle of the human soul. However, some Muslims, particularly the radical ones, offer a second interpretation—that of the outer, physical struggle against the enemies of Islam."

"So, what does the name 'Bab al-Jihad' mean?" Kianna spoke up, the dark skin of her forehead wrinkling in curiosity.

"According to the Hadith, which are not part of the Qur'an but are supposedly traditions and sayings of the prophet Muhammad, there are eight doors through which believers may pass to enter into paradise, or *Jannah*. The founders of the city viewed the portals that bring people here as 'doorways,' and like the citizens of Elysium, they saw Tartarus as a kind of hell, or *Jahannam* in Arabic. So, they named the city after one of the doorways to heaven, hoping that someday the portal within the city will be reversed so they can return to earth. Bab al-Jihad is the doorway for those who enter paradise by participating in jihad."

"Well, that's comforting," Xavier said with a grimace.

"Can we move this along?" Charon asked sourly. "I don't see why any of this is important."

Raptor's gaze pierced into Charon's as he spoke. "It is of *extreme* importance. You all need to understand that Imam Ahmed and his followers are a minority, but they hold the power within the city. They enforce a strict adherence to *sharia* law, which is a legal system based on the Qur'an and Hadith. They are...religious zealots who won't think twice about dying for the sake of their faith...," Raptor said, his expression becoming blank as his voice trailed off. Forcing his attention back to the present, he continued. "Although foreigners are not uncommon in the city, they're watched closely and treated with distrust. The imam also has loyalists everywhere. If any of you are seen, you can be sure he'll know about it within hours."

"Can't we just use the holographic masks that we used to enter the Welcome Center back in Dehali?" Kianna asked.

Raptor shook his head. "The only reason they worked then was because no one would ever expect someone to want to sneak into a Welcome Center. If we had tried the same trick in any buildings of military or strategic importance, we would've been caught before we crossed through the front door. In Bab al-Jihad, however, the military is paranoid and have installed devices all over the city that will raise an alarm if a holographic mask is detected."

"Then how do we move about the city without being detected?" Jade asked.

An enormous grin split Xavier's features. "Why, the old-fashioned way, of course." Reaching into one of the shopping bags, he pulled out a long piece of black clothing and a box containing several types of makeup. "With disguises!"

2

RESCUE AT THE RAVINE

"Disguises?" Charon echoed. "What kind of disguises?"

Raptor's level of irritation reached near-explosive levels. One of his best friend's character traits that bothered him the most was his stubbornness when it came to the art of subterfuge. "If you're with us, Charon, then you're with us all the way. Xavier is going to use the makeup to make him, you, and Braedon look Arabic. Kianna and Jade will just wear *burqas*."

"What?" Jade said, her tone leaving no doubt in anyone's mind that she was completely opposed to the idea. "You mean that long black robe and veil? Uh-uh. No way."

"Yes way!" Raptor commanded, his voice taking on a definite edge. "Any woman walking around in public in strict Islamic society without at least a *jilbab* or *abaya* would immediately attract attention, much less a Chinese woman. At least with a *burqa*, your whole face will be covered with this lovely fine mesh, so we can't see your eyes. They're just too noticeable. So, you either wear it, or Xavier gets to turn you into a man!"

Xavier grinned at the thought. "Yeah! That'd be fun! I've got a couple of fake beards right here!"

After casting a vicious glare at the man, Jade snatched the black clothing out of Raptor's hands. Opening the left side door of the Spelunker, she exited the vehicle in defiant silence. Her pet *mindim*, Zei, confused by the sudden action, launched into flight after her. As Jade slammed the sliding door behind her, Xavier turned toward Raptor. "Well, you called that one right."

"Get started," Raptor said to Xavier, completely ignoring his last comment. "Start with Braedon. The sooner you're finished, the sooner we can get going." Without another word, Raptor left the vehicle and headed off toward where Jade now stood near the edge of the slope.

"You got it," Xavier said, mostly to himself. Opening the passenger door, he climbed out of the vehicle, then opened the right side door. "Charon, you and Kianna might want to get out and stretch your legs. This is going to take a little time and I'd prefer if you didn't interrupt me while I'm working. Braedon, sit here on the edge of the doorway so I can see better."

The three others followed the con man's instructions without comment. Once Braedon was in place, Xavier began applying the dark foundation to the man's face and hands. Kianna, who stood next to Xavier, opened up the other bags of items Raptor had purchased and began rummaging through them.

"So, where did you guys come up with all this stuff? Fake facial hair and stage makeup aren't exactly common purchases at most stores."

"Raptor had me compile a list shortly after we left Dehali," Xavier explained as he continued to alter Braedon's complexion. "He used his implant to TeleConnect with one of his contacts so that the stuff would be here when we arrived."

"And how is it that you know how to use this stuff so well? Were you in theater or something?"

Xavier paused and turned his attention toward her, an expression of sheer woundedness on his face. "I can't believe you truly don't recognize my face! Didn't you ever see *One Day Beyond Tomorrow* or *The Last StarCrosser*?"

Kianna frowned as she searched her memory. "Holovids? You were in those? Wait...wait a second. I *did* see *One Day Beyond Tomorrow*. Which character were you?"

Stunned, Xavier turned to stare at her before a huge grin suddenly spread across his handsome features. "Finally, someone who has actually *seen* one of my vids! Don't you remember? I was Derrick Morse's partner...the guy who gets killed by that rampaging *tunrokla!*"

"Oh yeah!" Kianna said with extreme enthusiasm. Seeing the exaltation on Xavier's face, Kianna could contain herself no longer and burst out in laughter. "I'm just messin' with you! I never saw either of those."

Xavier froze in place, his excitement slowly transforming into a mixture of amusement and sarcasm as he realized he'd been fooled. "Nice one. You got me good. I'll have to keep my eyes on you. Braedon, stop laughing so I can finish up."

As Braedon struggled to contain his laughter, Xavier returned to his task.

Raptor strode quietly over to where Jade was standing near the edge of the slope, the lights from the Spelunker casting long shadows on the far wall of the chamber. The thin, athletic woman was standing in silence watching Zei flit among the various rocks of the ravine, chasing small lizards that scurried to and fro to escape the winged predator.

"She sure is an energetic little thing," Raptor said as he drew near, his own gaze fixed on the small mammal. "You never did tell me how you managed to tame a *mindim*."

Without turning to look at him, Jade replied. "After I left New China, I came across some young men who had captured her and were...making a sport out of causing her pain. I confronted them and told them to leave her alone. As usual, they didn't listen. They also paid for their disobedience in blood."

Knowing her skill at hand-to-hand martial arts, Raptor guessed that the young men she mentioned probably limped away from the confrontation, if they left under their own strength at all. Taking a deep breath, Jade continued. "After I rescued her, I nursed her back to health. I tried to release her back into the wild, but she seemed to have formed a bond with me and wouldn't go. After a year, I made the bond even more permanent by implanting her with a communication and video chip. She was my sole companion for many lonely years..." Her voice trailed off as Zei glided back toward her and finally came to rest on her arm. Absentmindedly, she began stroking the gray fur, causing a contented squeak to escape from the animal's mouth.

Turning around, Jade faced Raptor before speaking again. "Look, Raptor, I know we've had a sort of...partnership for the past five years, and I'm grateful for the acceptance I've received from you, Charon, and Xavier. I consider you my friends... probably my *only* friends. However, there's a lot you still don't know about me."

Raptor returned her gaze, his expression serious. "Trust me. I get it. We all have our secrets."

Zei climbed up to her usual perch on Jade's shoulder as she lifted the *burqa*. "This...this simple piece of clothing... represents something that I've struggled with for many years. Something that triggers dark memories." For a moment, Raptor could see the deep pain that lay hidden beneath her hardened exterior. However, she quickly replaced her mask—her emotions once more in control. "Don't worry, I'll wear it when necessary. But *only* when necessary."

"That's all I ask," Raptor replied with a smile. "And right now, it *is* necessary. We'll likely get stopped at a checkpoint just before we enter the city. The men will search the Spelunker, and so we'll need you to have it in place well before then."

"Understood."

Thankful that his team was falling into line, and still mulling over what Jade had told him, Raptor turned and headed back toward the Spelunker, leaving Jade to her own thoughts. However, before he had taken more than a dozen steps, a low rumble that came from beneath their feet began to rise in volume. Before he could even call out to the others, the ground started to buckle and turn under him, causing him to lose his balance. As he fell, he heard a scream coming from where Jade had stood just moments before.

Raptor landed hard on his side, temporarily knocking the wind out of him. Fighting against the pain of the impact, he raised his head and tried to see what had happened to Jade. Although he couldn't see her, he did see Zei fluttering near the slope's edge, chirping in agitation. Raptor struggled against the shifting rock beneath his feet and was forced to use his hands to maintain his balance as he slowly made his way toward the edge.

Raptor, Charon, someone...please...help me! I'm...I'm sliding down...

Jade's cry came through the implanted computer chip in his brain. Although the voice was not audible, the creators of the TeleConnect technology had figured out how to fool the brain of the receiver into thinking it truly had heard the sender's voice, including inflection and tone. And Raptor knew instantly by the tone of Jade's call that she was in serious trouble.

Concern for his companion sent a renewed burst of energy through Raptor's body. Ignoring the small rocks of the cavern floor as they cut into the flesh of his hands, he moved closer and closer to the ravine.

Jade, I'm coming! Hold on! Raptor replied through the TC. The worst of the quaking appeared to be over, but he knew that it would only be a matter of time before aftershocks occurred. Reaching the edge of the ravine, he peered down the slope and felt his stomach lurch in fear.

The tremors of the earthquake had sent Jade over the steep edge. She had slid down several feet and managed to grab onto the corner of a large rock. Blood trickled down her dirt-streaked temple from a jagged gash near her hairline. She clung desperately to the hard stone, paralyzed with fear. Surprised by the intensity of her emotions, Raptor glanced around in confusion. He knew from past experience that the ravine wasn't deep enough to cause Jade serious injury even if she fell.

It was then that the first wave of heat and steam washed over his body.

Suddenly, the terrible truth hammered at him, causing him to reel as his own fear coursed through his trembling limbs.

The earthquake had opened up a fissure at the bottom of the ravine. Slowly, like a predator approaching its helpless prey, a small stream of hissing and oozing lava began rising up from the newly-formed cracks in the earth.

"Jade! Jade, can you hear me?"

For several heartbeats the woman remained unmoving. Finally, her eyes lifted upward toward Raptor, recognition slowly seeping its way through her dazed mind. "I…I can't hold on…," she managed, her voice weak.

Lying down on his stomach, Raptor found a handhold on another large rock just over the edge of the slope and lowered himself down feet-first until his arm was fully extended. Reaching out with his left hand, he called once more to Jade, who was now within arm's reach.

"Quickly! Take my hand!" he called, even as his eyes glanced over her shoulder at the rising lava that was even now less than ten feet below his friend. "Hurry!"

Gathering her courage and strength, Jade reached out her right arm toward Raptor, her fingers brushing his. However, the maneuver caused her grip on the rock to slip. Snatching her hand back, she tightly wrapped her arms around the stone just in time. Her feet scrambled for purchase on the loose dirt and small rocks beneath her, sending a cascade of debris down the hill and into the clutches of the hungry molten rock at the bottom of the ravine.

"C'mon, Jade! Don't you give up on me! Try again!" Raptor called out, his throat beginning to burn from the steam that rose up toward him.

For the first time since they had met, Raptor saw tears well up in Jade's eyes. The expression on her face sent his heart plummeting. *Rahib,* she said through her implant, using his real name, *promise...promise me that you will...you will find my sisters in New China. Help them...*

Raptor's heart began to beat wildly with anguish and dread as Jade's fingers began to lose their strength. Helpless to save her, Raptor felt tears of his own stream down his face. "No...," he said weakly.

Suddenly, a blue glow bathed Raptor and Jade from above. He glanced up in surprise and watched as the giant form of the Spelunker hovered over them. Under normal circumstances, the pressure from the gravity generators that kept the vehicle floating over the ground would have crushed anyone unfortunate enough to be caught under them. But the designers of the Spelunker built it for travel in an underground world full of unpredictable terrain. In addition to the main generators, the Spelunker came equipped with a collection of a dozen long, thin arms that extended out from the front, back and sides of the vehicle, each ending with its own miniature gravity generator. Like the legs of a spider, the extremely sturdy metal arms, which were about six inches in diameter, allowed the vehicle to "climb" over holes while staying upright by applying force to walls or slopes.

As Xavier maneuvered the vehicle slowly down the incline, Charon opened the side door. "Right there, Xavier! Just a little lower!" he called out as he reached out an arm toward Jade.

"I'm trying!" Xavier called out in frustration. "I can't go any lower on the slope itself. I've already got half of our legs dangerously close to the lava!"

"Lower me down!" Braedon urged as he climbed toward the edge of the door. Without arguing, Charon braced himself against the sides of the door and grabbed Braedon's right arm. Swinging over the edge, Braedon reached down to where Jade hung desperately to the rock on the slope and grabbed her around the waist. Still stunned from her head injury, she used the last of her strength to hold on to her rescuer. "I've got her!" Braedon called out. "Xavier, take us back up!"

Instead of fighting to climb into the vehicle while in this precarious position, Braedon instead walked cautiously up the steep slope as Xavier eased the Spelunker back toward the top of the ravine. Once they were safely on level ground, Charon released his hold on Braedon, then leapt out of the Spelunker to help Raptor, followed by Kianna, who ran to help Jade. A moment later, they were all safely inside the hovervan as the legs retracted slowly back into the body of the vehicle.

While Raptor and Kianna cleaned and dressed Jade's wounds in silence, Xavier hurriedly finished applying the makeup to Charon and Braedon, all the while keeping an eye on the lava, which appeared to have leveled off. After that, they all changed into their appropriate garb and Xavier gave Raptor a false beard. With most of their preparations complete, Xavier finished applying his own disguise as Raptor directed the Spelunker back onto the main road to complete their mission. Despite their near brush with death, the group felt a sudden urgency to get to the city.

The group drove the last twenty minutes in silence, their tensions rising as they observed more and more signs of the earthquake's destruction. Several times they were forced to slow down to avoid debris from portions of the tunnel that had collapsed. Finally, as they rounded the last bend, Raptor sucked in his breath at the sight before him.

The city of Bab al-Jihad was burning.

3

DEVASTATION...AND HOPE

Overwhelmed by the sight before them, Raptor disengaged the computer driver, pulled the Spelunker off the main road, and brought it to a halt. For several minutes, he and the others could only stare at the chaos that had enveloped the city.

The tunnel they had just exited sat high up on the enormous cavern that housed the city, giving them a perfect view of the carnage below. Of the eight entrances into the city, three appeared to now be blocked. The primary entrance, which lay on the other side of the cavern, was in ruins. Several of the huge, stone columns that lined the main roadway had fallen over, making travel nearly impossible, while large piles of rubble and debris covered two of the smaller entrances.

The city itself was in even worse shape. In addition to the occasional collapsed building, the violent tremors broke numerous stalactites free from the ceiling of the cavern. The giant wedges of mineralized rock plunged into roads and complexes, causing explosions and fires to break out all over the city. Cracks and fissures dotted the cityscape, often with vehicles or even buildings sticking out of them. Black smoke billowed up from various locations to collect at the roof of the cavern. The thick plumes of darkness seemed at war with the rays of yellowish light that shot out from the center of the city's tallest structure.

"At least the Golden Dome still stands," Xavier commented. "The city's going to be hard enough to navigate through in the light. I'd hate to think what it would be like in pitch blackness." Although he had never been to Bab al-Jihad, he, like most citizens in Tartarus, was at least passingly familiar with the prominent features of each of the six largest population centers—and Bab al-Jihad's Golden Dome and its magnificent tower were certainly one of the greatest wonders in all of the underworld.

The tower sat in the exact center of the circular cavern. Beneath the intricately carved structure with its three balconies and the shining dome that capped it were several other elaborate buildings, including the largest and most beautiful mosque in the city. Adorned with arches, minarets, columns, and domes, the Baro Shona Masjid, or the Great Golden Mosque, was connected directly with the base of the central tower. A large, walled courtyard containing an exquisitely designed fountain in the center extended out from the back of the tower and was encircled by smaller structures used for storage, offices, and meeting rooms.

The entire complex containing the tower, the mosque, and the other six surrounding buildings were built upon a small island in the center of the cavern that was surrounded by a lake of silvery water. Four long bridges constructed of white marble connected the island to the rest of the city, which extended from the water's edge to the purple-hued stone that comprised the walls of the cavern. Each of the bridges pointed to a cardinal point of the compass, in essence dividing the lake into quarters. The northernmost bridge, and largest of the four, led to the now blocked main entrance to the city.

Throughout the cavern, sirens flashed as emergency vehicles drove rapidly to and fro in a frantic effort to bring order to the chaos. While the outward battle for calm raged below, Raptor sat above it all, fighting an inward battle against his own raging emotions. Paralyzed by shock and his own turbulent memories, he was finally brought back to the present by the slight pain of a heavy hand slapping hard against his right shoulder.

"Raptor! We need to get moving!"

The combination of Charon's words and physical nudge succeeded in penetrating the turmoil of Raptor's thoughts. "This is a perfect chance to enter the city! Look!" Charon said, pointing to an area farther down the road. "The checkpoint is abandoned! The guards must've been called away to help with the rescue operations. We can enter the city unchallenged!"

"Right...," Raptor said as the gears slowly began to turn in his addled brain. After putting the vehicle into drive once again, he manually steered past the wreckage on the street and headed past the checkpoint. Normally he would have chosen to use the large hoverlifts to take them down to the level of the city. But under the current circumstance, Raptor elected to use the winding road that hugged the walls of the cavern.

As they progressed slowly into the city, the sights and sounds of the catastrophe burned deeper into the fiber of their beings. Although the earthquake in Dehali had been strong, it hadn't caused nearly as much widespread destruction as the one that had just struck Bab al-Jihad. People filled the streets. Emergency crews fought to clear rubble and free those trapped in crushed buildings. Paramedics set up makeshift medical tents to help the wounded. Families stumbled through the streets seeking to find their loved ones, some grieving at their loss. Even the ten-foot-tall robotic war machines piloted by the Islamic militants were being conscripted to aid in the rescue efforts, their giant arms lifting heavy beams and debris.

Several times Raptor was forced to turn the Spelunker around to avoid areas of congestion or heavy damage, and at other times he was only able to continue by using the Spelunker's gravity legs.

"So...where are we going, boss?" Xavier asked at last, his mind pushing back against the horror of the surrounding events.

Raptor waited several seconds before replying. "We find somewhere to stay. I had a place in mind, but we can't get to it now. The northwest corner of the city doesn't appear as damaged, so I'm heading there. I know a couple of hotels that we can use, if they have vacancies."

"At least we shouldn't have to worry too much about being seen," Charon stated. "With all the chaos and so many needing a place to sleep, we shouldn't have a problem blending in with the crowd."

"What then?" Braedon asked from the backseat. "What's your plan for getting Gunther and Travis back?"

The entire group was silent as they waited for Raptor to respond. "I've got an idea, but I need to see if...I need to meet with a...friend first. I'll have more answers after that."

The group traveled in restless silence for the rest of the trip. At last, an hour after the earthquake hit, Raptor brought the Spelunker to a halt in front of a middle-class hotel in a section of the city that appeared relatively undamaged. Despite the current crisis, he managed to book two adjoining rooms for the group. Dressed in their new disguises, they carried all of their belongings into their rooms without incident.

Emotionally exhausted, Raptor and the others collapsed onto the beds and chairs of the rooms and turned on the holographic projector. With a mental command, Xavier transferred the images and information from his implant feed to the unit.

The group sat transfixed as they stared at the three-dimensional images of the enfolding drama as the rescue crews worked to free those trapped by the earthquake. However, after only a few minutes, Raptor stood and headed for the door.

Noting the worried lines creasing his friend's forehead, Charon followed him and stopped him just as he was preparing to step into the hallway. *Hold on a second, Rahib,* Charon said through a TeleConnect channel. *Where do you think you're going?*

Struggling against his emotions, Raptor had to fight to keep his thoughts focused. *Caleb, you saw the holos. I've got to...I've got to see if she's okay.*

Yeah, I figured as much. I'm assuming you've already tried to TC her?

Yes, but since she doesn't have an implant, I had to try her signal translator. She's either got it turned off or the earthquake did something to mess up the signal.

Okay, but if you plan on going alone, you'd better figure out a way to knock me out or tie me down!

To his surprise, Charon's comment actually succeeded in breaking through his friend's dour mood, causing a faint smile to crease Raptor serious expression. *Fine. But you'll have to wait in the Spelunker just in case her husband is around. I don't want to raise any alarms.*

Whatever. At least you'll know I've got your back if you need me, and I can keep an eye on things for you. So, unless you feel the sudden urge to bid a personal farewell to the others, let's get going.

The two stepped fully into the hall and allowed the door to shut behind them. As they walked toward the Spelunker, Raptor sent a brief TC message, his eyes losing their focus momentarily. *Jade, Xavier, we'll be back in a few hours. Get some rest, and no matter what happens, DO NOT let anyone leave the hotel.*

"Braedon, look here."

Before turning to see what Kianna wanted, Braedon glanced through the open doorway that led into the adjoining hotel room. Jade appeared to be asleep on one of the beds, and Xavier was engrossed in watching the newsfeeds. Satisfied that he and Kianna could talk freely, he crossed the room to where she sat at the work desk. Sitting on the edge of the bed, he gazed at the holographic screen that hovered above the device. "Have you found something about my wife?" he whispered.

"Yes. I think so. When we didn't find anything in the traffickers' records about who they sold her to, I thought we'd hit a dead end, especially since they likely changed her name. But then I got the idea to try a different angle."

Braedon frowned as he stared at the display. "What are these? Some kind of...public documents?"

"Marriage certificates," Kianna confirmed.

"But how does that—"

"It dawned on me that the traffickers who sell the women to the jihadist soldiers in Bab al-Jihad are selling them as brides!"

Braedon looked up from the screen. "How does that help us?"

She pointed toward another display. "The list we obtained from the Dehali Welcome Center shows the names of the women who came through the portal and were sold *and* the dates in which they arrived!"

"So if we know the date they arrived, and we know what marriages were performed around that time, we can narrow down who she was sold to!"

Kianna nodded. "There were one hundred and fourteen marriages performed in Bab al-Jihad within the ten days of her arrival in Tartarus. The way I see it, it would take them at least a day to process her arrival, another four days to get here, and another day or two for them to sell her, and for them to get the paperwork ready for marriage. So, we can exclude at least the first week. That drops the number down to sixty-seven.

"Look here," she continued. "There was a disproportion-ate number of marriages done within this two-day period! My guess is that this was due to the arrival of new victims."

"How many are we talking about?"

"There were twenty-three marriage certificates given out on those two days."

Braedon appeared defeated. "That's still too many. It would take us forever to investigate each of those. We just don't have the time."

Kianna placed a reassuring hand on his shoulder. "Don't give up hope just yet. I found something else. I was wracking my brain trying to come up with a way to find her, when I remembered that the two of you arrived in Dehali!"

"So? How does that help?" Braedon asked in confusion.

"Each of the portals in Tartarus is linked to specific loca-tions on earth, right?" she asked rhetorically. "All of the portals from earth's North American continent send people to Ely-sium, all of the ones that appear in the African continent send people to the United African Nations, the Asian portals appear in New China, et cetera. Although you were from the United States, since you and your wife were traveling through India at the time you were pulled through the portals, you arrived in Dehali.

"Well, with all of the new arrivals coming through the portals from earth," she continued, "many of the cities began keeping track of not just a person's arrival year, but also his or her *nationality*. I cross-referenced some of the names on the wedding certificates with cultural heritage and found that, as you would expect from victims from Dehali, nearly all of them were of Indian descent. All except one." As she finished speaking, she pulled up a file on the holographic screen for Braedon to read.

Suddenly, a mixture of relief, fear, determination, and rage struggled for dominance within the muscles of his face. "That's it! That's her! You found Catrina!"

4

ECHOES OF THE PAST

Raptor felt a sudden rush of relief as the mounting tension in his body drained away in a flash.

The house was intact.

"Charon, stop here," he commanded. The mercenary immediately complied, pulling the hovervan over to the side of the cracked concrete road. They had been driving for the better part of an hour. Much like the drive into the city, they were often forced to take detours to avoid the ongoing rescue and cleanup from the earthquake. "According to my information, her house is the fourth one on the right."

"So, what's your plan? Are you just gonna waltz right up to the front door and knock?"

"Pretty much."

Charon harrumphed. "And what if her husband answers? Don't you think he's gonna want to know why a strange man is asking about his wife?"

"If he answers the door, I'll just pretend to be a concerned citizen going door to door checking to make sure everyone is okay from the earthquake," Raptor replied as he opened the passenger door of the Spelunker. "But remember, her husband is former military. That means that in a crisis like this, he's probably been called in to help."

"I hope for your sake you're right on that. I've already saved your sorry hide enough times for one lifetime."

With a grin, Raptor closed the door and started walking toward the house. His thoughts occupied elsewhere, he reached up and absentmindedly scratched at his fake beard. As he approached the main gate of the fenced-in home, he felt his heart thudding hard against his chest and his hands moisten with sweat.

Fighting through the mental and emotional chaos that enveloped him, Raptor suddenly regained his focus as he caught sight of the tiny niche in the brick fence post that revealed the telltale signs of a security camera. Pushing aside his feelings, he forced himself to fall into his role of concerned citizen. He pressed the intercom button as his forehead creased in mock concern and fear. "*Asalaam Alaykum.* Hello? Anyone there?" he called out in Arabic, putting a bit of extra tremble in his voice.

A moment later, a muffled female voice replied through the intercom. "*Wa 'Alaykum Asalaam.* What do you want?"

Although the voice was muffled, Raptor instantly felt his pulse quicken. He was right. This was indeed the correct address, and the fact that her husband had not been the one to respond could only mean that he wasn't home. Swallowing hard, Raptor dropped his act and let his features soften. "Zahra, it's me. Rahib."

Raptor remained rooted to the spot, his heart beating loudly in his ears. He had thought about this moment for many years, but had often wondered how she would respond. Would she welcome him in, or reject him and send him away? Finally, after what seemed like an eternity of waiting, he heard the lock release and the gate retracted into the brick wall. A second later, the front door of the house slid open. Walking rapidly down the path, Raptor arrived at the door just as a woman stepped out onto the terrace, her thin frame dressed in a black *jilbab* with beautiful blue, red, and silver shapes surrounded by gold bands around the cuffs and hem. The long, flowing garment covered her entire body except her feet, hands, and head, which was surrounded by a richly embroidered, teal *hijab*. Her left hand held the corner of the elaborate headscarf across her face as a veil, leaving only her eyes visible.

But those dark brown pools spoke volumes. Shock, anger, fear, pain, anguish—all pierced Raptor's soul with such intensity that he found himself gasping for air. "Rahib? Is it...is it really you?"

Stunned by her presence, Raptor's lips struggled to form the words. "Yes...yes, it's me."

Shaking off her own momentary paralysis, Zahra glanced hurriedly down each side of the street. "Quickly! Come inside before anyone sees you!" Doing as she commanded, Raptor stepped into her house, his mind reeling.

Even before he could take in the luxurious furnishings of her house, Zahra closed the door, then threw herself into his arms, embracing him in a crushing hug. As he returned her affection, he suddenly felt her body shake in uncontrollable sobs.

For the first time since leaving home nineteen years ago, Rahib Ahmed felt his emotional wall slip. Despite his best efforts, tears slowly crept their way down his face.

Lost in the joy of their reunion, time seemed to stand still for the two of them. "Hi, *ukhti*," Raptor said at last as he felt her hold began to relax. She leaned back and spent a moment studying his features. Now that they were inside the house, she no longer held her *hijab* across her face. He stared in amazement at how his scrawny little sister had blossomed into a beautiful mature woman. "You look...you look so beautiful," Raptor stammered.

She smiled at the compliment, then reached up one of her delicate hands to touch his beard. "I see you've finally grown a proper beard."

Leaning back from her touch, he grinned faintly. "Actually, it's a false beard. I...I need to blend in while I'm here."

Like a bucket of cold water being thrown in her face, his comment brought Zahra back to the present. She shoved him hard away from her, the expression on her face darkening severely. "Where have you been? Since you ran out of our lives, you haven't bothered to visit even once! Or contact me more than half a dozen times. I wasn't even sure if you were still alive. And Father won't tell me anything."

At the mention of their father, a cloud of darkness passed over Raptor's face. "Just as well. It's a long story, and one I'd rather not talk about."

Frustrated, Zahra put one hand on her hip. "Then why are you here?"

Before he could respond, a young girl about eleven years old came into the room carrying a handheld device. She was so caught up in the image being displayed on the device that she didn't even notice Raptor. "Mom, look at this! The newsfeeds are showing—"

She stopped talking midsentence as she looked up for the first time and noticed the stranger standing in the doorway. Immediately, her expression changed from jovial to serious, her eyes dropping to the floor. "Forgive me. I...I didn't realize we had company."

"It's okay, Alina," Zahra said. "Mr. Hashim is my cousin."

Bowing slightly, Alina offered the traditional Islamic greeting. "*Asalaam Alaykum.*"

"*Wa 'Alaykum Asalaam,*" Raptor replied.

With the greeting complete, Alina looked up at her mother for guidance. Zahra gestured toward the room from which

Alina had come. Bowing again, the girl excused herself and exited back into the house proper.

"So that's Alina," Raptor said at last. "If she had answered the door, I would've thought I'd stepped back in time. She looks just like you did when I...when I left. By the way, thank you for...for not telling her."

Zahra shrugged. "And what would I have said? 'Alina, this is your uncle that you didn't even know existed.'"

"She doesn't know about me?" Raptor asked, his expression pained.

A sadness came over Zahra as she replied. "How could I tell her? Our father has forbidden mentioning your name. As the and caliphate of this city, our family's honor suffered greatly when you left. I haven't told Alina or Tarik about you."

"And how old is he now? Five?"

"Six."

"Does he take after you as well?"

"No. He looks much more like his father."

"Speaking of his father," Raptor began as he looked around the corner that led into the living room, "where is your husband?"

"He's out doing what every *good* Muslim man does in a crisis: he's helping those in need."

Raptor frowned at the less-than-veiled slight. "Yeah, well, I'm *not* a Muslim at all, much less a *good* Muslim. Besides, I'm not even sure there is such a thing."

His sister's expression left no doubt that he'd struck a nerve. "C'mon, Rahib. You know that most of us don't follow a radical interpretation of the Qur'an. How can you even say that?"

"I say it because I grew up in it. As did you. How is it that you've become so brainwashed that you don't see the violence inherent to Islam?"

"I haven't been brainwashed," she said, her tone defensive. "True Islam is a religion of peace, not violence. And no one is making me choose to believe. You know enough of the Qur'an to remember the Surah, 'There shall be no compulsion in religion.'[1]"

Turning away from her, Raptor walked over to the exquisitely carved bookshelf. On the highest shelf, just above his eye level, a leather-bound copy of the Qur'an sat in a golden bookstand. Although he no longer revered the religious text, the instructions that were ingrained in him from his youth on how to properly handle a written copy prevented him from touching it. As he spoke, he stared at the book as if he could peer through the cover and read the words of the text contained within. "Yes, except that particular verse was abrogated later by a newer revelation that says, 'I will cast terror into the hearts of those who disbelieve. Therefore strike off their heads and strike off every fingertip of them.'[2]" Turning back around to face Zahra, he continued. "It sounds like Allah changed his mind to me. You'd be surprised by how much I remember. I was an exceptional student of the Qur'an back then," Raptor said, his tone hard and sarcastic. "I know what it teaches. My instructors made sure I'd memorized the hundred or so surahs that dealt with how to treat the infidels. More important, I've seen the consequences of belief in those teachings."

"So have I," Zahra replied, her eyes glistening as tears began to form. "But instead of dwelling on the negative, I've found so much peace by focusing on the over *two* hundred verses that promote peace and compassion. Don't you remember what the prophet Muhammad, praise be unto him, once said after he returned from battle? 'We are going from the lesser *jihad* to the greater *jihad*,' meaning that living our daily lives is a greater struggle. He had so many wonderful teachings about love. Have you forgotten, 'Allah enjoins justice, and the doing of good to others'?[3]"

Raptor's eyes narrowed. "I wonder how those wives who are beaten by their husbands feel about that one." Zahra looked down, unable to withstand the intensity in her brother's gaze. "Yes, Zahra. I know your first husband took Surah 4:34 seriously. How can you believe Islam is a 'religion of peace' when you know how Muhammad treated women—how your husband treated you? This isn't some radical interpretation from an imam. This is straight from the Qur'an and Hadith! 'Men are in charge of women because Allah preferred some of them above the others... And of whom you fear rebellion, so preach to them and separate from them in the beds and *scourge* them.' That seems pretty straightforward to me!

"Or what about the story in the Hadith about the beaten and abused *believing* woman who complained to Muhammad —"

"—peace be unto him—" Zahra hastily added, interrupting Raptor.

"—and was told by him that she should return to her husband and submit to his sexual desires?⁴" he finished, ignoring the interruption. "And remember his words as recorded in Abu Dawud? 'A man will not be asked as to why he beat his wife.'⁵ *This* is the leader you revere?"

Zahra looked up at him, her eyes full of pain. "Why did you come here, Rahib? To remind me of my past and humiliate me? I don't understand why Allah would allow some things, but that doesn't change the fact that I trust in the truth of Islam."

Raptor stepped closer to her and took her by the shoulders, his face softening. "Is it in the past? Did the abuse stop after Arqam was killed in the *jihad*? How is your second husband treating you?"

A slight smile spread across Zahra's beautiful features. "Shafiq is a good man. He doesn't chastise me."

Raptor studied her face for a moment, searching for any signs of untruthfulness. Finding none, he relaxed and let out a sigh of relief and released her shoulders, a sudden flood of emotion washing over him. "I'm...I'm glad to hear it, although

THE TARTARUS CHRONICLES BOOK 3: BAB AL-JIHAD

I can't imagine how the imam would let you marry a man who didn't subscribe fully to his teachings."

Although Zahra's face reflected her concern at the fact that her brother chose to refer to their father by his title, she chose not to challenge the comment. "I don't think he realized that Shafiq had changed some of his once-radical views. Since I had already been married once, it was...harder for Father to find a suitable husband. I also believe that he didn't want to see me widowed once again, so he married me to an older man who would not be participating in *jihad*." This time, Zahra was the one who closed the gap between them and placed a hand on Raptor's right arm. "I know you haven't forgiven him for...for what happened. Despite what you think, he still loves me very much...as he does you. He only wants what's best for us."

At her words, all softness left Raptor, replaced by a white-hot rage. Pulling away from her, he turned his back and stared out the front window of the room, his eyes unfocused as his mind rebelled against him and retrieved the forbidden memory. When at last he spoke, his voice was icy and cold. "How can you still defend him?" he sneered. "Your faith in this religion has blinded you to the truth." Turning around, he glared at her. "Islam is just like all of the other religions! They're simply ways for clever men to control the gullible masses!"

The wounded expression on her face tempered his anger, causing him to pause before continuing. "I love you, Zahra. I wish you could understand how we were brainwashed as children. I've seen and experienced things that...Trust me—there is no God. This world of suffering is all there is."

His sister's look of sadness left no doubt in Raptor's mind that a huge gulf stood between them—a gulf that would likely never be bridged. The young girl he had shared a childhood with had become a woman, a wife, and a mother. The gulf had been created when he had left home. But now, their philosophical differences had widened the rift even further. Although they were bound together by a blood tie that could never be severed, his sister was nonetheless a stranger to him.

"Rahib, don't allow the actions of a minority to turn you away from Allah."

Raptor shook his head. "It isn't only the actions of his followers that have done that. It's also the *teachings* of his followers and his supposed prophet—"

"—praise be unto him."

Frustration at her devotion overtook him. "This is a mistake. I shouldn't have come here."

"Then why did you?"

"Because I wanted to make sure you and your family were unhurt after the earthquake."

Zahra appeared skeptical. "I appreciate your concern, but don't lie to me. You were already in or near Bab al-Jihad when the quake happened, and you wouldn't have come back unless it was urgent."

Despite his frustration, Raptor couldn't hold back the grin that forced its way onto his face. "Some things never change. You always did have a knack for seeing right through me." However, the grin faded almost as quickly as it had appeared. "Zahra, the truth is this earthquake wasn't an isolated incident. I'm sure you've seen the newsfeeds. This is happening all over Tartarus. And even more, the AAC is planning for war!"

Shock edged out all the other feelings that had been swirling within Zahra, leaving her numb. "How do you know?"

"It's a long story. But I...I've come because I need your help."

"Help?" she echoed in surprise. "Help with what?"

Raptor took a deep breath. "I need you to help me break into the imam's offices next to the Great Golden Mosque."

1. Surah 2:256
2. Surah 8:12
3. Surah 16:91
4. Bukhari 72:715
5. Abu Dawud 2142

5

UNEXPECTED AID

Shouldering his backpack containing his medkit, water, food, and his XR-27 laser pistol, Braedon moved silently toward the door of the hotel room. Stopping to glance in the mirror, he made sure his false beard and head covering were securely in place. Kianna came up to stand beside him and to take a moment to fix her *burqa*, which covered her from head to toe in black fabric so that only her eyes could be seen. In the adjoining room, Braedon could still see Xavier sitting on the side of the bed, his attention focused solely on the newsfeeds. Using his implant, he activated the sliding door that led into the hallway, which opened with a soft hiss...

...to reveal Jade standing right in front of them, Zei perched on her shoulder.

"Where do you think you're going?" she asked.

For a moment, Braedon froze. When he'd first met Jade back at the Crimson Liberty safe house in Elysium, she had quickly bested him in hand-to-hand combat. Even now in her weakened state, he was unsure that he could take her if it came to a fight. He let out a quick breath, hoping that it wouldn't come to that.

"Jade, listen. We found out back in Dehali that my wife is in Tartarus! She—"

"Yes, I know," she said, interrupting him. "Xavier may be too engrossed in the news to have overheard you, but part of the reason I've survived this long is that I've made it a point of always being aware of my surroundings…especially when I'm given specific instructions to make sure you stay put."

At this last statement, Braedon tensed. "I don't want to fight you, but I'll do whatever is necessary to rescue my wife!"

To his utter surprise, instead of her usual stoic expression, a look of compassion and empathy made a rare appearance on the Chinese woman's face. "I believe you. And you should save her," she said with conviction.

Both Kianna and Braedon paused in shock and disbelief. Finally, Braedon recovered his voice. "But…you said…What about Raptor's instructions? Won't he…"

"It won't be the first time I've disobeyed one of his orders. He's my partner, not my boss, even though I sometimes let him think he is just to boost his ego. Now tell me," Jade said, her demeanor becoming businesslike once more, "how do the two of you plan to get to her? From what I overheard, she's at least six miles away. Are you going to walk?"

Braedon glanced over at Kianna in relief. "We hadn't quite figured that out yet. Since neither Kianna nor I speak Arabic, it would be risky for us to try to take a taxi or public transportation. With the recent crisis in the city, we hoped maybe we could find an abandoned car with keys still in it."

"You goody-goody types are terrible when it comes to the subtle craft of espionage," Xavier snickered as he walked up to stand behind Kianna and Braedon. "And just for the record, Your-High-And-Mightiness, you're not the only one who can pretend to not be paying attention to his surroundings. In fact,

I've known that these two have been plotting together about something for at least…five minutes!"

Zei let out a loud squawk in response to Xavier's pretentious attitude.

"Now look, I'm all for this whole ride-in-and-save-the-damsel-in-distress thing," Xavier continued, ignoring the small mammal, "but don't you think it's a bit risky? Raptor told us to stay here, and that's just what we should do."

Jade appeared about to reply, but Braedon spoke first, his eyes burning with an inner fire. "I'm *not* going to just sit by for even one more second while my wife is being held against her will! If it was *your* wife, what would you do?"

Xavier's expression turned more serious, as if Braedon's question had struck a nerve. "Yeah, I get it. But I'm still not comfortable doing this without Raptor or Charon. As you've already pointed out, none of us even speaks Arabic."

Braedon shook his head. "No. I'm not even convinced Raptor would agree to try to rescue her at all. I'm going now, with or without your help."

Xavier sighed. "Fine. Do what you want. But if I were you, I'd just hotwire a car."

The comment caught Braedon by surprise. "Can you do that? I thought the manufacturers had figured out how to prevent theft."

Xavier shook his head, a triumphant look on his face. "That *was* the case. But during our brief stay at the Vagabond Hotel in Elysium, I ran into an old friend who taught me a new trick. With the right skill and knowledge, one can use an implant to hack into the car's computer!"

"Yeah, well, we don't have that particular skill set," Braedon replied sourly. "So unless you're offering to help us…"

The con man frowned as he saw a gleam of inspiration light in Braedon's eyes. *Xavier, I need your help on this,* Braedon said through the TeleConnect channel. *You owe me one for not telling Raptor that it was your mistake during that Pandora's Box session that told the imam's men that we'd be at the Dehali Welcome Center. I'm cashing in on that favor!*

Jade and Kianna watched the silent exchange between the men until finally a look of defeat came over Xavier as he finally acquiesced. "Fine, I'll help," he said aloud. "But I'm tellin' ya, Raptor ain't gonna be none too happy about this."

"I don't much care *how* he'll feel about it," Braedon stated. Turning his attention back toward Jade, he said, "Thanks for not making this harder than it needed to be."

Curious as to how he managed to convince the con man to help, Jade nevertheless kept her thoughts to herself. "Now that we're all in agreement, let's stop wasting time and get going."

"We?" Braedon echoed. "I don't need you to come along. Especially since you're wounded."

Jade's eyes narrowed. "You know, Braedon, your chivalry is quaint and somewhat charming, but it can also be annoying. It takes a lot more than a cut on my head to keep me down. I've got my own reasons for coming along, not the least of which is to keep an eye on you and dumb-nut over here," she said, pointing her thumb in Xavier's direction.

"Ouch!" Xavier exclaimed, looking hurt. "What did I do?"

Ignoring him, Jade continued. "I need to make sure you don't do anything to draw unwanted attention to yourselves. Speaking of which, I'm gonna grab my smothering 'black blanket,' then we can go." Without waiting for a reply, Jade reentered the room to change back into her *burqa* and get Zei settled. Once she was ready, the four of them locked the room and headed out of the hotel.

"Help me! Please help!"

The black-clad woman slammed her fists against the heavy metal gate as she waited for a response from the owners of the fenced-in home. Finally, after several seconds, a female voice responded through the intercom in accented English. "What is the matter?"

"My cousin's husband is hurt! We were on our way to help her family after the quake, but a car came around the corner and hit him! Please! His head is bleeding!"

The intercom was silent for several seconds. "Can you Tele-Connect the hospital to send an ambulance? Some of the feeds are inoperable, but the emergency lines are still working."

"We tried! But with the rescue operations going on, they can't get here for over an hour. Please! I need your help!"

"I'm sorry, but my husband is not at home."

The stranger cried out in anguish. "Please, have mercy! We need to get him off of the street! His wound is bleeding badly and I fear he will die! Please! You must help us!"

The com went dead, and for a moment, the woman thought the owner was going to refuse to assist. Suddenly, the large front door of the beautiful home opened and two women exited, both wearing colorful *jilbabs* along with matching *khimars*, or veils. As they opened the gate, the stranger pointed toward a couple sitting on the side of the road twenty feet away, the man's head cradled in the woman's lap. As the three approached, the man gave a soft groan. Although his wife's face was covered by the mesh of the *burqa*, her shoulders shook in grief.

With one look at the blood covering the man's face, the two newcomers immediately reached down and assisted the strangers in lifting the man. Before long, the four women had managed to carry him into the house. Once inside, they laid him down gently on a bed that was in a room not far from the entrance of the home.

"Ifza, go get some warm water. Quickly!"

"Yes, Binesh."

As the other woman exited the room, Binesh suddenly realized that the wounded man's wife was not with them. Puzzled, she turned toward her other guest. "Where is his wife? I thought she—"

Before she could finish her sentence, Jade stepped into the room, her black *burqa* draped over her arm. "It's all clear. I've done a scan of the house. There's no one else here but these two women, and one more woman who is taking care of three children under the age of ten."

To their host's utter shock and amazement, the wounded man suddenly opened his eyes and sat up straight. As she watched, the man took a cloth out of his pocket and quickly wiped away what she now guessed was fake blood from his head and face. However, her shock changed to fear when he stood and came toward her. Backing into the wall, she began to scream. Reacting quickly, he placed his hand over her veiled mouth, stifling her cry.

Dumbstruck, Binesh just stared at him as he spoke. "Shhhh. We're not going to hurt you. I'm sorry for the intrusion. Please, we need your help."

Before he could say more, Jade interjected. "Braedon, I'm heading back into the other room to keep an eye on the women and children. I'll also update Xavier on our status."

Still keeping his hand on Binesh's mouth, Braedon turned to acknowledge Jade. "Okay. I'll TC you when we know something." As Jade left the room, he returned his attention to the captive woman. "We're looking for someone by the name of Catrina Lewis. Do you know her? She's about five foot, six inches tall with red hair and green eyes."

Having removed her own *burqa*, Kianna walked over to stand beside Braedon. Placing a reassuring hand on the woman's arm, she smiled. "You might know her as Sabihah."

Seeing the recognition in Binesh's eyes, Braedon felt his heart skip a beat. "You know her? Please, tell us where she is. I'll let you go if you promise not to scream." The woman shook her head and relaxed slightly. Stepping back, Braedon removed his hand from her mouth. As he did so, her veil fell away to reveal an Arabic woman in her late twenties.

For several moments, Binesh remained stiff and rigid, as if paralyzed. Finally, she swallowed hard and took a deep breath before responding. "Who are you? Why are you looking for her?"

"I'm looking for her because she's...she's my wife," Braedon replied, his voice cracking from emotion. "She was taken from me years ago. Please, if you know where she is, tell me!"

Binesh studied Braedon for several seconds before making up her mind. "Yes...yes, I...I know her. She lives here with us. She is the one your friend said is with the children!"

Braedon felt his body tingle with excitement as tears filled his eyes. "Thank you! Thank you, Binesh." However, as he turned to leave the room, Binesh reached out a hand to stop him.

"But you don't understand. She is...she is my husband's favorite wife! Zarrar is very jealous and very protective of his property. If you take her, he will stop at nothing to kill you! He is a very powerful and vengeful man!"

Turning back toward Binesh, Braedon opened his mouth to speak, but was cut off by a sudden incoming implant connection. *Braedon, Jade—you've got company! A car with three men dressed in AAC uniforms just sped past where I'm parked and stopped in front of the house! And even worse, they're armed with Lexar Quad-lasers!*

6

DIVIDED LOYALTIES

"Break into Father's offices? Rahib, are you insane?"

Zahra stared at her brother as if he had suddenly sprouted wings and a tail. "Why would you want to do...wait. Please tell me you aren't going to steal something."

Raptor reached out and took her hands in his and guided her to the nearby couch where they both sat. "No, it's nothing like that. I have a lot to tell you, and I need you to listen carefully." Starting with his first meeting with Gunther and Braedon, Raptor filled her in on all that had happened to him in the last three weeks in Elysium and Dehali, leaving out all mention of Steven's prophecy, the two signs that would accompany it, including his nightmares, and his journal. Throughout the entire story, Zahra sat unmoving in shock and amazement. Once he had finished, she shook her head in disbelief and stood up.

"This is...this is just all so incredible!" She slowly pivoted to face him, her mind still reeling. "Do you...do you really believe all of this? I mean...do you think this Gunther can really reverse the portals? And...the earthquakes! How much time do you think we have before...before Jahannam collapses?"

Shaking his head, Raptor stood. "We don't know. Braedon's source didn't go into details, and the governments of Tartarus are keeping a tight lid of the data. Then again, after today, people are going to demand some answers. Quakes in Dehali, New China, and now here within one week? That's hard to cover up."

"But surely if Father knows about the danger, then we should try to talk to him. If you have this…Vortex weapon and he has the scientists who can use it to open the portals, then we should take it to him."

"No," Raptor said emphatically. "You don't know him as I do. Over the years I've made quite a few connections, and several of them have kept me informed about what the imam is doing. Don't you get it, Zahra? He's preparing for war! He wants *jihad*! He wants to follow in his father's footsteps!"

Raptor's sister looked down with a blank expression on her face, her mind focused inward. "No. He's not like our grandfather."

"I'm sorry, Zahra, but he's not the man you think he is. You're his daughter! Of course he isn't telling you everything. He wants to finish what his father started. He was thirteen during the War of 163 and had his head filled with visions of glory through religious zeal. He feels it's his *duty* to wipe out the rest of the citizens of Tartarus! If he gets the Vortex weapon, he'll likely use it as a weapon. And even if he doesn't, he'll only open a portal in Bab al-Jihad and let the destruction of Tartarus do his job for him."

Zahra sat back down on the couch, troubled by her brother's words. "Then…what do you plan to do?"

Raptor began pacing the room as he spoke. "We have to get Gunther and Travis back. From what Braedon and Xavier said, they were able to obtain the information they needed from the Dehali portal just before they were captured."

"And you're sure they're being held in Father's offices?"

"Yes," Raptor nodded. "It's the only place that makes sense. It's extremely well guarded, and, being on the island, it's difficult to access. Besides"—he paused—"you probably aren't even aware of this, but...when I was eleven, I stumbled upon a section of the complex that is used to...to interrogate 'infidels'."

The blood slowly drained from the beautiful woman's face, leaving it pale. "I...you saw it?" she stammered.

"Yes, although I never told anyone I knew about it," Raptor said.

Shaking off the disturbing news, Zahra pressed on. "But even if you somehow succeed in rescuing them, what then?"

"Gunther and Travis said that once they had the data, they would have to reprogram the Vortex, then use it on an existing open portal to finish the calibration. After that, they should be able to actually use the device to *create* portals back to earth."

"And where are you going to get access to an existing portal?" she asked. "The only one in the city is in the complex. Once you free the scientists, I don't think Father is just going to let you back in to access the portal."

Raptor stopped his pacing and turned to look at his sister, his expression creating in her a sense of foreboding. "Yeah, that's the tricky part. If we can't get to the portal in Bab al-Jihad, we may have to find another one."

"But where? Are you going to return to Dehali?"

"No. Both Dehali and Elysium are too dangerous at this point."

"So, New China, then?"

"Probably," Raptor lied as he strode over to the far wall of the room. Although it appeared he was studying a mosaic with the embroidered verse from the Qur'an that hung on the wall, his mind was far from the artwork. In truth, he knew that even if they were successful in rescuing Gunther and Travis, a trip to New China would take them past the deadline of Steven's prophecy.

"But I'll cross that fissure when I come to it," Raptor said. Leaving the artwork behind, he returned to the couch. "Zahra, will you help me? I need someone with security clearance to get me into the offices quietly, without raising alarms."

Raptor's sister looked away as she considered his request. Burdened with the weight of this new information, she stood and took several steps away from the couch before turning, as if the distance between her and her brother would lessen the pressure. "How can you ask this of me, Rahib? You're asking me to choose between two loved ones! I don't want to betray Father. If he ever found out....You know what he could do to me!"

Standing, Raptor quickly walked over to where she stood. "But he won't find out. All I need you to do is transmit the proper code via implant to the security system."

"But that would mean I would have to go with you, or the TC proximity detectors would know that I wasn't truly at the complex!"

"There are ways around those," he reassured her. "I have access to a relay box that would fool the system into thinking that the TC code was transmitted locally. And the beauty of using the implants is that there's no physical evidence to prove you were involved."

"But *I* would know."

"*Ukhti*, I'm not asking you to help *me* as much as I'm asking you to do it for your people! If this works, we can open the portals all over Tartarus. Hundreds of thousands of lives could be saved."

Reluctantly, Zahra nodded her assent, even as she looked down, the burden of the decision settling onto her shoulders.

"Thank you. I promise that things will work out. And then...then maybe I could finally meet my niece and nephew."

The corner of Zahra's mouth curved in a faint smile. "I'd like that. But only if you promise to never run away again."

"We'll see."

A look of sudden alarm leapt onto Zahra's face. "I lost track of time! It's nearly three thirty! They will be announcing the call to the *Asr* prayer time! You must hurry! My husband said he'll be home by then!"

Spurred on by her urgency, Raptor quickly headed toward the front door.

"Wait!" Zahra called, halting him in his tracks. "I want to give you something." Grabbing a white cloth from the nearby shelf, she reverently reached up with her right hand and pulled the leather-bound Qur'an from its golden stand. "Please. Would you take this? It is my personal copy, and it would mean so much to me if you would read it. Look for the *good* in Islam."

Moved by her sincerity, Raptor accepted the gift. Despite the fact that he no longer held any reverence for the holy book, he nonetheless made sure he took it and the cloth in his right hand for the sake of his sister. "Won't your husband notice it's missing?"

"We purchased identical copies. I'll replace mine with his. He rarely reads it, so it shouldn't be missed. Besides"—she smiled—"it's only a short-term loan. You're going to bring it back to me in a week or so when this is all over, right?"

Raptor returned her smile. "Right. I love you, *ukhti.* I'll TC you when we're ready."

"Can't you just give me your TC code so I can contact you?"

His smile faded. "I'm sorry. Not yet. It's not that I don't trust you, I just…if you don't know it, you can't be forced to reveal it to others."

A hint of fear returned at his statement. "I understand. Someday you'll have to tell me all about what you've been doing during these past twenty years to turn you into someone so cautious."

"Not a chance," Raptor replied seriously. "There are some things best left unknown. *Khuda Hafiz,* Zahra." Without another word, he hurried out the door. Within moments he was through the main gate, disappearing once more from Zahra's life and leaving her with nothing more than memories.

7

CATRINA

Wait! Braedon, Jade—they're splitting up! Two are coming in the front door, the other one is heading around the back. I'm on my way, but the gate may slow me down. Reacting instantly to Xavier's TeleConnect message, Braedon grabbed his backpack that had been deposited next to the bed and urged Binesh and Kianna toward the door leading back into the main living area. Sensing that something was wrong, both women complied willingly. As they moved, Braedon explained the situation.

"I don't know how, but it seems that your husband knows we're here," he said to Binesh. "He and two friends just arrived, and they're armed. We need to get you to someplace safe." Leading them into the kitchen, Braedon came to a halt as Jade hurried up to them.

"I've sent the women and children to the basement," she announced.

"Good. Kianna, I want you and Binesh to head down there as well," Braedon commanded. Needing no further prompting, the two women immediately disappeared through a nearby door, their footsteps on the stairs fading quickly away. "Jade, cover the front entrance. I'll take the back."

"Move over," she said as she took out a laser pistol from a holster that hung down across her right thigh. Stepping to the side, Braedon watched in surprise as she pointed it toward a small crease between two cabinet doors and pulled the trigger, blasting a small hole into the wood.

"What was that all about?" Braedon asked as he reached into his backpack and retrieved his own blaster.

"When I scanned the house, I found hidden cameras in each of the rooms," Jade explained. "Now that this Zarrar knows we're here, he can no doubt access the camera feeds through his implant. You have to take out the cameras first or he'll know our every move. There are two in that back living area: the one on the left is lodged in the vase on the shelf, the one on the right is in the frame of the mosaic on the wall. Good luck." With her weapon held in front of her, Jade darted around the corner toward the front of the house. A moment later, Braedon heard two more shots from her pistol as she took out more of the cameras.

Within moments, Braedon had reached the room in the rear of the building. The large recreational room was filled with several couches and chairs arranged so that they could easily see the images from the holoprojector mounted on the ceiling. Large windows that stretched nearly from floor to ceiling offered a spectacular view of the expansive, well-manicured backyard. Two glass sliding doors led out onto a wooden deck.

Taking up a position at the edge of the hallway leading into the room, Braedon took aim and quickly disposed of the cameras. With that accomplished, he found a new defensible position behind a nearby couch and waited.

The two Arabic men entered the home cautiously through the front door, their rapid-fire, four-barreled blasters leading the way. With military precision, they fanned out and advanced, each one covering the other as he moved. They made it to the entrance of the dining area and halted, one on each side of the wide archway.

For several seconds they remained frozen in their current positions as they visually scanned the room for signs of the intruders. Their eyes immediately focused on a still form dressed in a black *burqa* that was sitting in a chair at the far end of the table and slumped facedown on it. After making eye contact with each other, one of the men nodded toward the other. Keeping his weapon trained on the other archway leading out of the room, the lead soldier crept toward the figure at the table.

With his attention divided between the exit and the still figure, he never saw the attack coming.

Jade let go of the wall-climbing suction devices she attached to the opposite side of the archway and landed silently behind the first man. His partner attempted to adjust his aim toward the unexpected attacker, but Jade kicked the weapon out of his hand before he could fire.

Hearing the scuffle behind him, the first man spun around. Ducking low, Jade swept his feet out from under him. Even before he crashed to the ground, Jade leapt forward on top of the second man just as he was diving for his weapon. Abandoning it, the man twisted under her, sending her rolling to the side. Completing the roll, Jade came up to a crouch to see that the other attacker had recovered and was nearly in firing position.

Snatching her pistol out of its holster, Jade sent a volley of several shots in his direction, the third blast of energy finally hitting its mark. However, her initial lack of aim gave her remaining opponent enough time to get back to his feet. Using his larger and more powerful body, he drove the small woman into the floor and pinned her facedown. Grabbing her black ponytail, he lifted her head and prepared to slam it into the ceramic tiles.

The crack of a laser blast split the room, startling both combatants. A second later, Jade felt the pressure on her back suddenly ease as the man slumped to the floor next to her. Looking up in surprise, she saw Xavier standing in the doorway of the house, his pistol pointing in her direction.

Letting out a sigh of relief, Jade pushed herself off the floor and stood. "What took you so long?" she snarled as Xavier moved quickly over to join her. "A moment longer and I would have a broken nose!"

Xavier stared at her in irritation. "You know, I just can't win with you. A couple of months ago when you got into a scrape with those three drug-pushers, you got mad at me for ruining your fun by taking out two of them for you. Now I get to the fight just on time and you bark at me for being late! Sheesh! You're worse than this woman I used to date. She would—" He stopped midsentence as he suddenly caught sight of the figure slumped over at the table. Walking up to it, he lifted the *burqa*. As he pulled out the pillow that was stuffed inside it, he glanced over to see Jade retrieving her climbing devices. "Ah, so you pulled the old draw-their-attention-then-drop-from-above trick. Very nice. I remember when Raptor used that on—"

His words were cut off by a far off scream that erupted from below them. Jade glanced at Xavier, the intensity in her eyes boring into him.

"C'mon! We've got to get to the basement!!"

Kianna and Binesh rushed down the steps leading into the basement. Reaching the bottom, they turned to the left and entered a spacious room that had clearly been set up as a children's play area. Dolls dressed in Muslim attire and toys of various kinds were stacked in bins against the wall. On the far end were two book-shelves containing children's books, and reading chairs.

Binesh led the way through the playroom to a door along the wall next to the reading area. Opening it, the Arabic woman led Kianna into a storage room full of shelves of food and small crates with lids. Standing among the shelves were three fright-ened children and their two equally frightened caregivers. Kianna recognized the first woman as the one that helped bring Braedon into the house—the one Binesh had called Ifza. As the second woman looked up at her, Kianna could see strands of reddish hair sticking out from her *hijab* that were accented by her green eyes.

She had found Braedon's wife.

As Binesh closed the door behind her, Kianna walked slowly forward as if approaching a wild animal that could bolt at any second. "Catrina? Catrina Lewis?"

The woman's fear slowly melted into confusion. When she spoke, her voice sounded hollow, as if coming from far down an empty tunnel. "How...how do you know my real name? Who are you?"

Kianna let out a sigh of relief at the confirmation, as well as a silent prayer of thanksgiving. "My name is Kianna. I'm a friend of your husband. Your *real* husband."

"Braedon?" Catrina managed, her shock robbing her voice of its strength. "Where...where is he? Is he...is he alive?"

Fighting against tears that sprang unbidden to her eyes, Kianna nodded. "Yes! He's here! He's just upstairs."

A war of emotions broke out suddenly on Catrina's face. Joy and hope fought desperately against fear and despair for con-trol of her mind. However, just as hope was beginning to gain a foothold, the sounds of laser shots came from the living area above, causing fear to emerge triumphant within her.

Surprisingly, the children remained silent and calm, causing Kianna to wonder briefly what horrors they had been forced to grow accustomed to. "Everything's going to be okay," she soothed, hoping her own uncertainty didn't show. "We aren't going to hurt you." The sound of the door opening behind her caused her to turn...

...just in time to see a large Arabic man standing in the doorway, his laser pointed at her face.

Reaching out, he grabbed Kianna by her dark-brown hair and yanked her head back. "Who are you people and why are you in my house?" he commanded in thickly accented English.

"I...we are...we were looking for someone," she stammered.

Not satisfied with her answer, the man forced her to her knees and put his gun against her temple. "Who were you looking for? Tell me now or I will teach my children how they should treat enemies of Allah!"

Kianna cried out in pain as the man forced her head back farther. However, before she could even respond, Ifza spoke up, answering the question for her.

"Zarrar, they were looking for Sabihah! This woman claims that she has another husband who is upstairs!"

Zarrar's eyes flared with outrage and betrayal. Throwing Kianna to the floor, he released her and turned toward Catrina, who shrank back in terror. Grabbing her by the throat, he lifted her to her feet. "You...you lied to me!" he said through gritted teeth. "You told me you had never been with a man!"

Eyes wide with fear, Catrina gasped for air as the man's left hand began to close around her neck. Cursing violently, he pulled her out of the storage room and threw her toward one of the chairs in the reading area. Catrina tripped and let out a scream of pain as the arm of the chair dug into her side. Collapsing on the floor facedown, she began to weep uncontrollably as Binesh, Ifza and the children stood watching helplessly, their faces devoid of all emotion.

Wild with rage, Zarrar holstered his weapon and stood over Catrina's crumpled form. Grabbing the back of her collar with his right hand, he yanked her up and used his other hand to backhand her across the side of her head. Dazed, Catrina backed away from him until she bumped up against the bookshelves, her *hijab* coming loose, allowing her wavy red hair to spill out of confinement. Begging softly for mercy, she raised her arms up in front of her face as she saw his right hand curl into a fist.

But before the blow could fall, the sound of hurried footsteps descending the stairs penetrated the haze of vengeance that had overtaken Zarrar's mind. Snatching up his blaster once again, he spun around and unleashed his fury. The Lexar Quad-laser rotated and spit out a continuous stream of laser bolts that tore into the wall of the stairwell.

When his target did not emerge, Zarrar reached down and pulled Catrina up to stand in front of him as a shield. "Come out now or I will kill her!" he bellowed as he placed his weapon against her head.

Braedon, still wearing his fake beard and *keffiyeh* headscarf, slowly rounded the corner of the wall and entered the room, his hands held up in surrender. As his gaze fell upon his wounded wife, he felt a sudden surge of emotion, with injustice and revenge dominating all others.

Confused by his disguise and disoriented from the cut to her head from Zarrar's blow, Catrina seemed resigned to whatever fate was about to befall her.

"Drop your weapon!" Zarrar snarled. Reluctantly, Braedon complied. With his opponent now flushed out into the open and unarmed, Zarrar's thirst for revenge at this invasion of his home flared up once more. Switching targets, he pointed his blaster toward Braedon and prepared to pull the trigger, a wicked grin of triumph twisting his face.

Pain suddenly exploded in Zarrar's arm as Kianna brought a heavy broom handle down upon it, causing him to drop his weapon. Bellowing in rage, he threw Catrina away from him and turned toward this new attacker. Filled with a fury of his own at the sight of his wife being tossed aside, Braedon launched himself at the man and tackled him to the floor.

Backing away from the two combatants, Kianna noticed that Binesh, Ifza, and the children were still watching the struggle from inside the storage room, their expressions filled with uncertainty. Grabbing the handle of the door, Kianna closed it quickly before returning her attention to the melee.

With his martial arts training, Braedon landed several heavy blows against the man's head, stunning him. However, even with Zarrar subdued, Braedon felt himself losing control at the sight of Catrina's bloodied and battered body. Leaping to his feet, he left the dazed man and strode over to retrieve his pistol. Flipping the setting back to lethal, he lifted Zarrar and slammed him up against the wall and placed the gun against his chest.

Kianna, shocked by Braedon's actions, called out frantically to him. "Braedon, stop! What are you doing? This isn't right! Don't do this!"

Breathing heavily, Braedon felt his finger tighten on the trigger as Kianna's words slowly pierced his mind. From the dark places of his soul, he heard a voice encouraging him. *Do it! He deserves it! He is the enemy! He was going to kill you!* Then, like a gentle breeze blowing away a fog, Braedon heard a second voice whisper to him. *You shall not kill. Vengeance is mine, I will repay.*

The still, small voice continued to repeat itself until it drowned out all other thoughts. Coming to his senses, Braedon released his hold on Zarrar and took a step backward. As he did so, Zarrar raised his head, his battered face full of spite. "You are weak! A true warrior would finish his enemy! And know this: if you let me go, I will hunt you down and make you watch as I take your lecherous woman and—"

A laser bolt split the air, tearing a hole through Zarrar's chest and cutting off his final words. As his lifeless body crumpled onto the floor, Braedon, Kianna, and Catrina turned in shock to see Jade standing just inside the room at the bottom of the stairs, her laser pistol pointed at the dead man.

8

REPERCUSSIONS

"Jade, what did you…why did you do that?" Kianna asked, the horror of what had just transpired still raw in her mind.

The Chinese woman casually holstered her weapon, her face cold and uncaring. "He was too dangerous to be allowed to live. We're going to have a hard enough time trying to rescue Gunther and Travis as it is without this filth raising more alarms."

"But…but he was unarmed," Braedon said, his own frustration barely contained.

"In case you hadn't noticed," Jade stated, her anger flaring, "he was just beating your wife and threatening to *kill* her! What's wrong with you, Braedon? All I did was made sure he'll never lay a hand on another woman again."

A muffled voice abruptly ended the conversation. "Braedon? Is that…is it really you?" Turning toward the crumpled form of his wife, Braedon suddenly felt all strength drain out of his legs as he saw for the first time in nearly ten years his wife's green eyes staring back at him.

Collapsing on the floor in front of her, he took her face gently in his hands. "Yes, Cat! It's me!"

Her eyes roved back and forth as she studied his face. "But… you look so…so different."

Remembering at last that he was still wearing the false beard and makeup, he smiled in spite of the turbulent emotions swirling within his breast. "It's a disguise!"

As if realizing for the first time that she wasn't dreaming, Catrina burst into sobs of relief and joy as she threw her arms around her husband and wept. The reunited couple, lost in each other's embrace, became oblivious to the others in the room. Swept up in the drama of the moment, Kianna, Xavier, and Jade stood motionless, bound by some unseen holy presence that permeated the atmosphere of the room.

Finally, after an indeterminate amount of time, the storage room door opened slowly, instantly reminding the group of the unfinished business that lay ahead of them. Reacting immediately, Kianna stepped up to the door to stop Binesh from opening it farther.

"Wait! You can't come out yet! The children…"

The Arabic woman's eyes grew wide as they fell upon the body of her dead husband. Reeling in horror, Binesh cupped her hand over her mouth and drew back into the storage closet. As she did so, Kianna narrowed the opening and whispered, "Give us a few minutes. We'll let you know when it's safe to come out."

Closing the door fully, Kianna turned to see Jade emerging from around the corner of the stairway. "There's a laundry room on the other side of the basement. Let's get this over with."

Together, she and Xavier quickly moved Zarrar's body around the stairway and into the other room. As they entered, Xavier's attention was caught by the slight fluttering of curtains near a small open window about two feet tall and three feet wide. Following his gaze, Jade swore as she released Zarrar's body, letting it fall to the floor.

"That's how the scumbag got in. Jade, you're an idiot," she admonished herself.

"What's wrong?" Xavier asked in surprise as Jade turned and left the room to rejoin the others. Snatching a folded bedsheet from a nearby shelf, he hurried to follow her.

Once back in the play area, Jade strode over to where Braedon and Catrina were now standing. "There's an open window in the laundry room. I'm afraid it's my fault he came down here first," she said.

"What do you mean?" Kianna asked, her brow furrowing in confusion.

"I knew he had access to the security camera feeds, so Braedon and I took out the ones upstairs. Although that slime knew what area of the house we were in, I figured he wouldn't know our exact locations. But it didn't dawn on me that he would also know where we *weren't*. He came after you, probably wanting his wives and children to leave the house through the window while he went upstairs to get the drop on the rest of us."

Braedon looked down at Catrina, thankful that things hadn't turned out differently.

"But what I don't get is how did he even know you were here in the first place?" Xavier asked. "Ol' boy and his crew came screaming down the street and bolted out of the car like rabbits on speed!"

Catrina squirmed at Braedon's side. "I...I sent a TC message to him when you first arrived. It's what he commanded us to do if ever he isn't home and anyone, especially a male, comes to the door."

"But how'd he get here so fast, and with friends?" Xavier asked. "Does the guy *always* leave home with his trusty Lexar Quad-laser in his hand, and with a couple of spares just in case his buddies need them?"

A pained look came over Catrina's face. "Actually, he does. Zarrar, Fahad, and Othmane are all part of the army. When the earthquake hit, they were ordered into the streets near our home to keep the peace."

"That reminds me, what happened to the other two?" Braedon asked.

"Jade and I took care of them," Xavier said as he tossed the bedsheet he had collected onto the floor to cover all remaining traces of the skirmish. "Speaking of which, we should probably head upstairs and move them out of the way as well. But before we do that, what do we do now? I mean, what about them?" he said with a nod toward the storage room.

"We leave them," Braedon said, his emotions conflicted. "I don't know what else we can do."

A sudden sense of urgency and fear overwhelmed Catrina, causing her to inhale sharply and grasp her stomach in pain. "We've got to leave now!"

Startled, Braedon stared at her in concern. "What is it?"

Taking a deep breath, Catrina continued, her body beginning to shake. "Although Zarrar was often cruel, Binesh and Ifza were loyal to him. They have likely already contacted the AAC!"

Realizing their danger, Jade and Xavier bolted up the stairs, Braedon and Catrina close behind. Spinning around to face the storage room, Kianna called out to the women and children still huddled inside. "Binesh, Ifza, we're almost finished. For the sake of the children, please stay in there a few more minutes." Without waiting for a reply, she ran up the stairs.

Two minutes later, Xavier pulled their borrowed vehicle to the back entrance of the house. Once the five of them were inside, he drove quickly away. Turning the nearest corner, he slowed down to a normal speed so as not to attract attention. Then, after four more blocks, he came to an intersection where the residential streets joined the main flow of traffic. Just as he was turning, the rear mounted cameras on the vehicle showed four military vehicles speeding down the street that led to Catrina's former residence and prison.

Braedon and the others arrived back at the hotel, exhausted and drained. Opening the door to one of the two rooms, they stepped inside and were greeted by Raptor and Charon, both wearing identical scowls of anger and disapproval.

Raptor swore harshly as they entered the room. "Where have you been? I distinctly remember giving the two of you explicit instructions not to leave! You could have—Wha—? Who is that?" he stammered as Catrina entered behind Braedon.

Without flinching, Braedon gently helped her remove her black *burqa*. "Raptor, Charon, I want you to meet my wife, Catrina."

For several moments, all either of the two men could do was stand and stare in shock. At last, Raptor found his tongue, his rage contained only with supreme effort. "And where did she come from?"

"Kianna and I discovered that she had arrived in Tartarus years ago and was sold by underground traffickers to a man in Bab al-Jihad. We tracked down his residence and rescued her."

Raptor's scowl deepened. "Oh, I see now. You jeopardized the lives of everyone in Tartarus so you could run off and play hero."

Braedon's eyes narrowed. "I did what I had to do to save my wife!"

Raptor glared at each of them. "Do you think I told you to stay here because I've got some…irrational need to control people? No! I did it because we're trying to keep a low profile! If the imam finds out we're here, then it'll be nearly impossible to rescue Gunther and Travis! And in case today's earthquake wasn't enough of a reminder, if we can't rescue one of those two and get them to calibrate the Vortex, then everyone—*everyone in Tartarus*—is going to die!

"And on top of that, there's also the possibility that the Guardians are still out there hunting for us! But instead of sitting quietly here while I get the help we need, you steal a car, break into Zarrar's home, kill him and his two friends, and take his legal wife!"

"Technically, we only borrowed the car," Xavier corrected. "We returned it completely undamaged thanks to my—wait a second. How did you know all that?"

"Because it's all over the blasted newsfeeds, you idiot!" Charon blurted out, his anger causing the muscles in his neck to bulge.

"But...how did you know it was us?" Xavier asked in confusion.

"It's not hard to put two and two together," Raptor spat. "When we arrived back here and you were all gone, we checked the news. Although most of the coverage is still about the earthquake, the murder of a prominent military commander and two of his men as well as the abduction of his wife by a group of four unknown assailants is a big enough story to catch people's attention. Now the whole city's looking for you!"

"We're not children, Raptor!" Jade fired back. "We've been doing this long enough to know how to cover our tracks. We scrubbed the scene of our fingerprints, ditched the car a long way away from here, made sure we avoided the city cameras, split up, and we had Braedon and Xavier switch into other clothes along the way."

"Yes, but you left witnesses! Now the imam will know for sure that we're in the city!"

"Oh, c'mon, Raptor!" Jade said, not backing down. "You're fooling yourself if you think he doesn't know we were at least headed here. His men took Gunther and Travis from us. He knows we're likely to come for them. In fact, has it ever occurred to you that he might be trying to lure you back here?"

"Yeah, I have thought of that. But now he knows *for certain* that we're here, which means he's going to be extra cautious. So thanks to all of you, our job just got a whole lot harder!"

Although shorter than Raptor, Jade's steely gaze and defiant posture seemed to make her grow larger. "And what did you want us to do, Rahib? Just leave her? How would you feel if it was *your* wife, or *your* sister?"

Jade knew she had hit a nerve as Raptor's frown deepened. However, since he didn't seem inclined to respond, she continued. "How could Braedon ever live with himself knowing that his wife was nearby being abused and not doing anything to help her?"

"He should have waited until we rescued Gunther and Travis," Raptor shot back. "We could have come back to rescue her later!"

Braedon suddenly became aware that Catrina had started to breathe heavily and had placed her hand on her stomach again. Wanting to comfort her, he reached out to put his hand on her shoulder. However, she jerked back instantly, as if his hand were a poisonous snake about to strike.

"Don't touch me," she snapped at him and backed away.

Her outburst didn't go unnoticed by the others. "It looks to me like she doesn't even want to be here or be with her hero."

Braedon glared at Raptor, the intensity of his stare like a predator ready to pounce. "You have no idea what she's been through!"

"Actually, I do!" Raptor retorted, raising his own intensity to match Braedon's. "Don't forget, I grew up in this culture."

"Then you know why we had to rescue her!" Jade interjected.

Raptor stared hard at Jade, his lip curling. "What's it to you? You don't even know her. Why do you care so much what a husband does with his property?"

The blow came so fast that Raptor hit the floor before he felt the pain in his abdomen. A thick silence fell over the entire room as Jade stood over him, her fists still clenched. "I care because I know what it's like to be treated like 'property'!" she stated coldly, her voice raw with emotion. "I was a trophy for seven years—smiling at parties and playing the faithful wife. But behind closed doors, my husband treated me like a slave!

"I eventually got my revenge" she said, her voice dropping even lower. "I found a teacher to secretly teach me martial arts. And one day..." Her eyes lost their focus as the memories washed over her. "One day, I couldn't take it anymore. I fought back and...and they had to take him out of the house in a body bag. That was the day I left New China."

Snapping back to the present, she looked down at Raptor as he slowly rose to his feet, his own anger completely evaporated by Jade's confession. "I escaped that life, Rahib. But my two sisters still face a similar fate. *That* is why I care about Catrina. And *that* is why *I* killed her husband."

"I'm sorry about your past, Mingyu. I never knew. I get why you did it, but it doesn't change the fact that it puts us in a bigger mess." Turning toward Braedon and Catrina, he winced and cupped his hand over the spot where Jade had hit him. "It's nothing personal. I'm just...there's something about being back in this city that's...It's just the pressure of what we're facing."

Acknowledging the semi-apology with a slight nod, Braedon turned back toward Catrina, who was still recovering from her near panic attack. "Now, if you don't mind, it's been a long day and Cat and I have a little catching up to do."

Together, the couple stepped through the opening between the rooms, then closed the adjoining door behind them.

In the awkward silence that followed, Raptor crossed over to sit gingerly on the bed, his side still throbbing. "Jade, remind me never to get on your bad side again." Still recovering from her heightened emotional state, she ignored the comment and sat down in a chair near the corner of the room.

"So, now that we've got all that settled," Xavier said hesitantly, as if testing the emotional waters, "how was your trip? Successful, I presume?"

"Yes, mostly," Raptor replied.

"Then what's our next move?"

"We'll talk about it as a group in the morning. For now, I want to make *sure* you weren't followed. You, Charon, and I are going to find a nice, quiet spot to set up watch. You take the north entrance. Charon, watch the south side. I'll take the main western doors. While we wait, I want you both to use your implant translators to monitor the military transmissions and newsfeeds for any hint that they know we're here."

"Sounds like fun," Xavier stated with mock enthusiasm.

"Kianna, since you obviously seem to know your way around the city's computer systems, do some snooping and make sure nothing pops up that would lead anyone to our doorstep. And I'm sure I don't have to remind you not to get caught."

"I'm already on it," she said as she pulled out her portable computer and powered it up.

Moving his focus to the final occupant of the room, Raptor said, "Jade, get some rest. I've got a feeling we're going to need you to be on top of your game in the next few days." From where she sat in the corner, he could barely make out the slightest nod of her head. Turning away from the rest of them, she looked toward the curtained window, a single tear sliding gently down her face. As he studied the Chinese woman's silhouette, he realized how little he had known about her past—or how much pain she carried within her.

Adjusting the *keffiyeh* wrapped around his shoulders and head, Raptor headed toward the door. Without a word, the three men left the room, leaving behind the two women, and the burdens they carried.

9

REUNITED

As the door closed with a gentle click, Braedon felt the tension in his body ease. They had done it! They had rescued Catrina, made it back safely, and confronted Raptor and Charon. *Why, then, do I somehow feel that the true battle is just beginning?* he wondered. Turning around, he saw that Catrina had moved over to sit in the lone chair near the desk in the corner, her head down and her eyes staring vacantly at the carpet.

"Hey," he said lightly, snapping her out of her daze, "I'm gonna get rid of this disguise and clean up a little. I'll be right back." He threw her a brief smile, then stepped into the bathroom. A few minutes later, he returned to the main room.

Catching sight of his familiar close-cropped hair and clean-shaven face, Catrina smiled weakly at him. "It really *is* you. You look so much more…mature."

"Thank you," he replied with a slight bow. However, as he held her gaze, her smile evaporated and she looked away quickly, her body rigid and tense.

"What's wrong?" Braedon asked. When he took a step toward her, she began to breathe rapidly as panic overcame her. Stopping immediately, he raised his hands up in a gesture of surrender. "It's okay. I…I'm not going to hurt you. Look, I'll… I'll just sit over here on the floor against the window."

Leaning his back against the wall beneath the window several feet from her chair, Braedon let out a sigh of relief as he watched Catrina visibly relax. Making himself comfortable, he offered up a silent prayer as he considered what to do next.

For nearly an entire minute, neither of them spoke. The quietness of the room acted as a balm to Catrina's nerves. Finally, her gentle voice broke the stillness. "Braedon, I'm…I'm sorry. I just…need some space right now. I'm still having a hard time believing that this is real. When I woke up this morning, my life was the same cruel existence that I had known for the past ten years. And now…I'm scared. I want to hope that things will be better, but I'm afraid to believe. I don't know if I even know *how* to hope anymore."

Now that they were in the relative safety of the hotel room, Braedon felt the adrenaline fading from his system. As his survival instincts faded, they left behind the tumultuous emotions of a wounded husband. Although the longing to hold her caused him to ache inside, he knew that she still needed time to process all that had happened. "If it makes you feel any better, I'm still struggling to believe this is real, too. I know what it's like to lose hope. I had lost all hope of ever returning to earth or seeing you again. And yet…here you are. I still can't believe that you were in Tartarus all along."

Her uncertainty evaporated and was replaced by a sudden flash of anger mixed with extreme pain and rejection. "Yes! I've been here for the past ten years! Why didn't you come for me? I watched and waited every day for that first year, believing that you'd come rushing in and save me from my living nightmare. But you…you never came…" Her words were choked off as she began to weep. "Why didn't you love me enough to find me?"

His resolve to keep his distance was broken by her grief. Getting up off the floor, he knelt down in front of her on one knee and reached out his left hand toward her shoulder. As his hand made contact, he felt her stiffen as her crying abruptly ceased. "Cat, didn't you hear what I said? I didn't know you were in Tartarus! They...they told me at the Dehali Welcome Center that I had arrived alone! I just found out four days ago that the men who run that center traffic women to Bab al-Jihad. They drugged us while we were still disoriented from arriving through the portal. They took you away and told me I had arrived alone! If I had known you were here, I would have spent every waking moment looking for you!"

Sensing that she was uncomfortable with his touch and his proximity, he removed his hand from her shoulder and leaned back on his left foot. Again, it took several moments before she responded, as if her mind was slowly chewing over his words to determine whether to swallow and accept them or spit them out like poison.

When she spoke at last, her voice was hollow and her green eyes were vacant once more. "I always thought watching my father hit my mother and older brother was horrendous. But that was nothing compared to what Zarr...to what *he* did to me and the others. I was given so many rules to follow, and if I forgot one of them, or he was in a bad mood, or even if he *felt* that I was being disrespectful in some way, he would..."

Braedon shook his head. "Don't say it. It's over now. He won't ever hurt you again."

"And the children," she continued. "The things he made them do and watch! He did everything he could to make sure his daughter would grow to be a compliant wife, and his sons would be just like him: cruel and hateful."

"Cat," Braedon said, trying to soothe her, "let's not dwell on the past. Focus on the good times that are coming."

She slowly turned toward him, a frown creasing her lovely face. "What 'good times'? From what your friend said, it sounds like either the military will find us, or the entire world will collapse. No, Braedon. There are no 'good times' for me. You shouldn't have rescued me. I'm cursed. You would have been better off leaving me."

Fighting against the frustration that began to build within him at her pessimism, Braedon took a breath before responding. "I don't believe that. You are *not* cursed. God has led me to you, and I believe he will help us open the portals."

"God?" she echoed, a hint of disdain coloring her voice. "God, or Allah, or whatever you want to call him, if he even exists, is cruel and spiteful."

"No, he isn't," Braedon said sadly.

"Since when do you...?" Catrina's expression suddenly shifted, a hint of fear creeping back into her face. "Are you...Do you believe in God now?"

He smiled, hoping to reassure her. "Yes. I do. Look, I know that neither of us was fond of religion during the three years that we were married on earth, but...but since coming to Tartarus, I learned things that convinced me that Christianity is true. But it isn't really about religion—which is just man's way of trying to get to God. Christianity is different. All other religions tell you what you must *do* to get to God. Christianity is about God *doing everything* to get to us!"

Despite the passion in his voice, his words seemed to fall on deaf ears. "Cat," he continued earnestly, "my relationship with God is nothing like what you experienced here."

"How? How is it different? All religions use rules and laws to subvert people and gain power. Christianity is just like the rest. You said so yourself, back when we first started dating. Don't you remember?"

Braedon smiled sadly. "Yes, I remember. I was a young fool back then. I thought I knew everything. But I'm not the man you once knew. The man you married was stuck up, self-centered, and pompous. C'mon, wasn't I?"

His question brought the slightest glimmer of a smile to her face. "Yes, you were quite a jerk at times."

"Which is why we fought so much. But...once I had everything familiar to me taken away, I was forced to take a hard look in the mirror. My mentor, Steven, helped me through the dark times when I first arrived. He helped me answer all of the questions and misconceptions I had about God and showed me how belief in Jesus is based on logic and reason, not on blind faith."

Catrina looked at him for several seconds, her expression a cross between skepticism and surprise. "I never thought I'd hear the words 'logic' and 'reason' used in the same sentence as 'belief.' You *have* changed, Braedon Lewis. And so far, I like what I see. You've certainly learned how to defend yourself. You used to hate confrontations, and I've never seen you move as fast as you did earlier."

"Yeah, I've learned a thing or two. Steven was also my instructor when I joined the Elysium Security Force."

"Wait a second," Catrina said in bewilderment. "So this guy is a Christian *and* a soldier in the ESF?"

Braedon nodded, his smile fading. "Yeah, he was. I've never met a greater man."

"Was?" Catrina asked, noting the change in Braedon's demeanor. "What happened to him?"

"We reconnected about three weeks ago. He helped me and Gunther escape from a Guardian. However...another Guardian surprised us and killed Steven just before we could escape from Elysium."

Catrina reached out a tentative hand and placed it over her husband's. At her touch, Braedon looked deeply into her green eyes and noticed a hint of the young woman he had married so many years ago. The spark of life had become ash and dust within her. Yet, the smallest ember still remained.

Rising up to her level, Braedon placed his hand gently on her cheek and leaned forward. Their lips had barely met when Catrina pulled away and turned her head abruptly to the side.

"I'm...I'm sorry," she said through a veil of tears, her voice quavering in fear. "Please don't be angry with me. I...I will do whatever you want."

Her words pierced his heart with grief and sorrow. "Cat, I would never...I'm not angry with you. I'm not like that."

Shame at her reaction was compounded by the rest of her tumultuous emotions. "Of course...I just...I'm sorry. So much has happened. I need more time."

Longing to hold her but recognizing her need for space, Braedon withdrew. "It's okay. I understand." Standing to his feet, he began to turn away but stopped as he felt her hand on his arm.

"Please don't leave me," she whispered. "I...I need you, but I just...I just need a little physical space."

Braedon struggled inwardly, his desire to put her needs before his own eventually winning out. "I know that so much time has passed, that I have to earn your trust once again. But I want you to know that I'll do whatever it takes—no matter how *long* it takes—to prove to you that I love you, and that I only want to see you healthy and whole.

"So," he continued, his expression taking on a lighter tone, "for tonight, I'll stay close here on the floor, as long as Kianna and Jade don't mind. This is their room after all."

"Thank you," she managed. "I don't deserve the kindness you and your friends have shown me. You shouldn't waste your time on me."

"Nonsense," Braedon countered. "Don't ever say that. Listen to me: you are worth it. You are…you are so beautiful, Cat. In fact, I think you're more beautiful now than you were when we first met."

Catrina smiled weakly once again. Embarrassed and ashamed by his attention, she changed the subject quickly. "Why don't you tell me about all that's happened to you? I want to hear more about Steven and your time with the ESF. I also want you to tell me everything that you've gotten yourself into."

Happy to oblige, Braedon made himself comfortable on the second bed and motioned for Catrina to sit on the other one. Once they were settled, he began his story. Within a matter of minutes, the two became engrossed in conversation. After several hours, Braedon noticed that his wife had finally drifted off to sleep. Glancing at his watch, he suddenly realized what time it was, and that the others had obviously chosen to give the two of them the privacy they needed.

Climbing off the bed, Braedon leaned over his wife's sleeping form and kissed her forehead. *Thank you, Lord, for bringing her back into my life. Please grant her peace tonight, and help her heal. Father, give me patience and make me into the man she needs and deserves. And, most of all, help me to point her to you and to your grace.*

The words of his prayer were still in his mind as he finally laid his head on the pillow of the second bed. Moments later, the stress and anxiety of the day gave way to the gentle peace of sleep.

10

PRISONERS

Gunther Lueschen felt the soft grass beneath his feet as he walked. The rays of the sun warmed his skin. Nearby, the gentle murmurings of the small river blended with the chirps, squawks and scurrying of the forest animals. A gentle breeze ruffled what remained of his graying hair.

He stopped as he suddenly took note of a bench that sat along a gravel path ahead of him. A lone figure sat motionless on the bench facing away from him. The figure had long gray hair that came to the middle of the back and wore a bright yellow dress spotted with pink flowers. Although he couldn't see the person's face, he felt the strange sensation that he had been here before. He knew this person.

Confused, Gunther continued walking toward the bench. As he approached, the bench's occupant turned her head toward him.

"Ah, there you are. For a moment I thought you'd gotten lost."

Gunther felt his stomach clench and his pulse quicken in sudden recognition. "Eveleen?" Overwhelmed at the sight of his wife, he quickly closed the gap between them and moved around the bench to face her. Reaching out tentatively, as if fearing she would disappear upon touching her, Gunther took her hands in his own. Emotion washed over him at the feel of her familiar, aged hands until he could no longer stand. Falling to his knees, he placed his head on her knees and began to weep. "Oh, Eveleen! It's really you! I thought I'd lost you forever. I'm...I'm so sorry! It's all my fault!"

Still sitting on the bench, Eveleen stroked her husband's thin hair, her wizened features softening with compassion and love. "It's okay, my love. I understand."

Raising his head, he stared at her in anguish, his eyes red and full of remorse. "No. No, you don't. It's all my fault. I should never have gone with Erick into the woods. I should have listened to you. It's my fault we got pulled through the portal. It's my fault Erick died. Don't you understand? It's all my fault! So many have suffered because of my mistakes. I don't deserve to live!"

"Don't talk like that," she chided. "My love, it is you that doesn't understand. There is a greater plan and purpose at work. You'll see. Don't give up hope."

Confused by her words, Gunther looked around him and noticed the forest for the first time. "Where are we? This isn't... this isn't Tartarus. How...how are you here?"

"You're dreaming, dearest. Complete the work you were sent to accomplish and return to me."

Rising to her feet, Eveleen began walking down the path. Although every part of him screamed to stop her, he seemed unnaturally paralyzed and could only watch helplessly as she moved farther and farther away. Finally, just before disappearing around a cluster of trees, she turned back toward him and whispered, "I'll be waiting..."

"Allahu Akbar."

The words of the *adhan* burst forth from the speakers installed in the ceiling of the room, causing the occupants to jolt awake for the second time that morning. Disoriented, Gunther stared at the ceiling, Eveleen's final whisper still ringing in his head. Sitting up, he glanced at his surroundings. The cold, gray walls of his prison cell and the sight of his companion brought the past day's events rushing back to him.

Sitting up in his cot on the other side of the small room, Travis ran his hand through what remained of his curly, red hair. He looked over at Gunther, his left eye black and nearly swollen shut from being struck with the butt end of a rifle. For a moment, the two men remained silent as the voice over the loudspeaker continued the call to prayer.

"I don't know how they do it," Travis said as he pulled his legs out from under the covers and swiveled them over the side of the cot. "I don't think I'd mind the praying five times a day if the first one wasn't scheduled before normal people even get up in the morning. I mean, they don't even turn up the Golden Dome until after the first one. Can't they even sleep in one day a week?"

Still clinging desperately to the last vestiges of his dream, Gunther was slow to respond. With supreme effort, he finally managed to force his brain to awaken. "Sorry. I…I just…I was dreaming."

"I hope it was about someplace nicer than this. Never mind. It wasn't important anyway. I was just complaining about our 'wake-up call.' I don't mind if people want to pray, but five times a day?"

"Good Muslims take it seriously. It's the first of the five 'pillars' in Islam. It's mandatory."

"Well, I wish they would at least take more time," Travis said, and he stood up and began to get dressed for the day. "It takes me usually twenty minutes to get going in the morning, and that's with coffee in my system. But if yesterday is any indication, they'll have finished washing and praying, and be waiting at our door in about half that time!"

Gunther sighed. "Welcome to Bab al-Jihad."

As Travis predicted, their cell door burst open just over ten minutes later. Immediately, Gunther felt his stomach lurch as his anxiety spiked. Four men entered the cell, rapid-fire laser rifles slung over their shoulders. One of the men tossed some fruit and bread onto the floor and began yelling at the prisoners in Arabic.

Travis, having learned through a painful jab to the eye not to argue or try to talk to the guards, reached down carefully and retrieved the food items. Handing some to Gunther, the two men stared at the dirty, stale food for a moment. As he considered his options, a painful rumble in his stomach reminded Gunther that he hadn't eaten in over a day. Fighting against his own revulsion, he forced the food down.

Before either of them could even finish their meager breakfast, the soldiers grabbed their arms and forced them to their feet. Shoving them hard in the back, the soldiers forced their prisoners out of the cell, down a drab stone hallway, through a series of secured doors and into the workshop. Wincing in pain from where the nose of the weapons had dug into their backs, the scientists sat down at the workstations that had been prepared for them.

"Good morning, gentlemen."

Turning toward the speaker, Gunther and Travis watched as Taj El-Mofty, the right-hand man to Imam Ahmed and top general of the AAC, stepped toward them. "The imam sends his greeting," he said in English. The man wore a white *taqiyah* embroidered with a repeating gold pattern. To compliment the rounded hat, he wore a knee-length gray tunic and white pants. The sleeves of the tunic contained a pattern of crisscrossing black lines and dots. His black, neatly-trimmed beard and mustache matched his dark complexion. Although he smiled at them as he approached, his deep brown eyes sent a contrasting message.

"I hope you rested well," he continued. "The imam wishes to stress that no more games will be tolerated. We know you can re-create the Vortex weapon."

"Games?" Travis echoed. "We...we don't know what you're talking about. We—"

El-Mofty cut him off with a wave of his hand. "Save your lies," he said through clenched teeth. "We are watching you always. We know you were stalling for time yesterday. So," he said, his countenance relaxing. "We thought we'd find a new way to motivate you."

Gunther glanced at Travis, then back at his captor. Suddenly, after all he'd been through, Gunther felt tired. Tired of trying. Tired of fighting. "Do what you want to us," he mumbled. "We won't work for you."

"Really?" El-Mofty said with a raised eyebrow. "Perhaps my news will change your mind." He looked coldly toward Travis, his face darkening. "I was told to inform you that we have your wife and children."

"What?" Travis yelled as he jumped to his feet. Responding to the sudden movement, the nearby guard backhanded him. Crying out in pain, Travis crumpled to the floor. With a nod from El-Mofty, two of the guards reached down, grabbed their captive by the arms, and deposited him back in his seat. Stunned, Travis simply shook his head as a sense of foreboding and defeat settled on his spirit. "Please, don't hurt my family! You're...you're right...we'll do what you ask. Just, please...don't hurt them!"

A satisfied smirk twisted the corner of El-Mofty's lips. "And you?" he said, turning his attention toward his other prisoner. "Will you cooperate also? If not, I have a couple of men who would be more than happy to welcome one of Mr. Butler's beautiful teenage daughters into their homes."

"No...," Travis mumbled through his split and bleeding lips. He looked over at Gunther, his eyes pleading for help.

"Yes, yes," Gunther said quickly. "You have our word. Just promise us that no harm will come to his wife and children."

Their captor bowed slightly, mocking them. "You have my word. Now that we have that cleared up, I'll leave you to your work." With another slight bow, Taj El-Mofty turned and exited the room.

With their tormentor gone, Gunther reached over and placed a reassuring hand on Travis's shoulder. "He may be bluffing. We have no proof that they really have your family. Raptor and Braedon are good at what they do. Sandy and the girls are probably still at the safe house back in Dehali."

Travis glanced over at his companion dully. "What does it matter? You know that even if we get to work right now, it'll take us months to re-create the research. If your hypothesis is correct, Tartarus will probably tear itself apart before we finish."

Gunther winced at the thought. "But at least we might be able to keep those monsters from harming your family. Besides, don't give up hope. As I said, Raptor and Braedon are good at what they do. They may even be planning a rescue at this very moment."

Deciding that their private conversation had carried on too long, one of the guards stepped up to them and spoke harshly in Arabic while motioning for them to get to work. Deciding not to push things further, the men complied.

Around them, several Arab technicians and scientists were already gearing up for the day's activities. As they worked, Gunther felt the presence of the two guards with high-powered laser rifles who stood on either side of the room's only door, as well as the ever-watchful eyes of the four cameras mounted on the ceiling.

Twenty minutes passed before Gunther found enough privacy to risk a second conversation. During that time, he had grown increasingly concerned about his friend's mental and emotional health. "Hang in there. Remember when I was going through those hard times dealing with Erick's death? You were always there to encourage me. You'd always remind me that there is a bigger story being told. 'The Celestials brought you here for a reason, Gunther.' Remember saying that? Hold on to that faith."

Travis turned slowly to face his companion, his swollen left eye completely shut now. "I don't believe that any more. You were right. There are no Celestials. There is no 'grand purpose' in life. We humans are on our own."

"But there *is* purpose: to love our families," Gunther whispered earnestly. "The one thing that has kept me going here in this accursed underworld is the hope of seeing Eveleen again." As he spoke her name, the image of her from his dream sprang into his memory, causing his eyes to brim with tears. "And you have Sandy and the girls. Let them be your purpose."

Travis raised one eyebrow questioningly. "Gunther, you're quite a contradiction. One minute you give me a philosophical rebuttal and explain why you think there is no God or Celestials that give purpose to life, and the next day you turn around and talk about love as the purpose in life. You can't have it both ways. Love only makes sense if we were created with a purpose."

For once, Gunther was thankful that one of the guards intervened and broke up their conversation. Travis's statement rocked him to his core and left him reeling for most of the next hour. Despite his previous conversations with both Braedon and Steven, Gunther had never really recognized the contradiction in his own thinking. *How come I've never realized it before?* he wondered. *I've always believed evolution to be true, but yet my emotions lead me in a different direction. I feel such intense love for Eveleen, but that love doesn't make sense in a purposeless world.*

Gunther and Travis continued working absentmindedly for the next couple of hours, their minds finding a sort of solace in the detailed work of reconstructing the Vortex weapon. On several occasions, the Arab technicians would approach them and discuss design instructions and plans.

Finally, just before the noontime call to prayer, one of the technicians approached the two men. "Mr. Lueschen, Mr. Butler, my name is Gorbat. I need to ask you about a couple of the specifications of the device in order to create the computer model."

Gunther nodded mechanically, his mind elsewhere.

Gorbat sat down next to them at the workstation. He laid his holographic projector on the desktop and turned it on. As his hands began to manipulate the image on the device, he spoke softly, catching the others off guard. "Keep your eyes fixed on the hologram as I speak. Don't look at me. Pretend we're discussing the device."

Surprised by the instruction, Gunther nearly did exactly what the man asked him not to do. Catching himself at the last second, he forced his gaze to remain on the hologram.

"Listen carefully," Gorbat said after making sure no one had taken a sudden interest in their conversation. "I came to tell you that your friends have arrived in the city."

"What?" Gunther said, fighting to keep his excitement under control. "How do you…how do you know this?"

For the sake of those watching, Gorbat stroked his bushy black beard and nodded as if he was responding to some bit of knowledge that the scientists had just imparted to him. "All I can tell you is that I know someone who is close to your friends. Just be ready to move when the time arrives."

"When will that be?" Travis asked.

Gorbat shook his head. "We don't know. It could be any minute, or it could take days. Just keep working. I'll let you know if we learn anything more."

"But what about my family?" Travis asked. "Taj El-Mofty said they were captured. I can't leave without them."

"I understand. I'll find out what I can."

Picking up the holographic projector, Gorbat pretended to study the data on the screen as he stood and walked away from their workstation. Turning toward Gunther, Travis gave him a mixed look of both hope and apprehension. "Do you think your friends will be able to help us? I mean, we're in the heart of the city. How could they possibly pull this off?"

"I don't know," Gunther replied honestly. "But if anyone can do it, they can. However, we have to keep our wits about us. For one thing, we don't even know if this Gorbat guy is telling us the truth. He could be working for the imam. Maybe he was sent to talk to us to get our hopes up or to befriend us. Be careful what you say to him, and take what he says with a grain of salt. We'll find out soon enough if he's telling the truth. In the meantime, let's keep your family safe by giving these scum some results to keep them happy."

Nodding in agreement, Travis threw himself back into his work. But despite his best efforts to focus, his mind kept conjuring images of his wife and children at the hands of these callous and wicked men, filling his heart with dread and despair.

11

CONTEMPLATIONS

Raptor awoke with a start, his heart pounding rapidly. His eyes darted furtively around the hotel room as if trying to convince himself that this was indeed reality. Coming fully awake, he swore under his breath as he relaxed onto the bed.

He'd had the nightmare again.

He closed his eyes. But when he did so, the image of the dragon's malevolent eyes and gaping maw leapt into his mind, as if it were simply lurking behind his eyelids, waiting for him to return to its realm of fear and pain. So instead of trying to return to sleep, Raptor stared blankly at the ceiling, his mind spinning.

It's getting worse. What's wrong with you, Rahib? You've never had the same nightmare multiple times. Are you really losing it this time? he wondered. *I've heard of people reliving traumas over and over, but a dark tunnel, a dragon, and a sword? What's with that?*

As soon as he asked himself the question, the unwanted answer forced its way into his thoughts. *You know where it's from. Steven said it was the first sign from God. Remember? He said it would haunt you to remind you of the truth until the end of your days. He somehow knew about your nightmare, just as he somehow correctly predicted that your life would be saved miraculously that very day! And if he was right about the two signs, then maybe...*

Raptor shook his head to break that train of thought. He wouldn't go there. And yet, despite his best efforts to ward it off, Steven's prophecy suddenly leapt into the forefront of his mind. Although he had never consciously memorized the words, he found that he somehow couldn't forget them.

This is what the Lord says:
You have cursed my name for many years,
And have despised those who speak my word.
Why? Because one you loved chose truth instead of lies,
Life, instead of darkness.

Now the lives of thousands rest in your hands,
Tens of thousands will live or perish by your choices.
Your fate is bound to theirs.
The days of your life are now numbered.

Only by opening the door to a new life
Will your own be saved.
You must seek out truth,
For only the truth will set you free.

The days of your life are now numbered,
They will be thirty and one!

As the words flashed through his mind, he felt an inexplicable fear paralyze his mind and body. *No! It's impossible! No one can predict the future,* he thought, desperately trying to convince himself. *It was just a coincidence that I survived that day. It wasn't God who saved me. And maybe Charon was right about Steven somehow planting the dreams in my mind. Someone is trying to manipulate me!*

He began to relax a little as his rationalizations began to take hold. But then, his own logical mind worked against his will. *But what are the odds that he could successfully predict that your life would be saved miraculously? What are the odds that a screwdriver would stick out of a grate at just the right angle and catch on your pant leg just enough to keep you from being pulled into the vortex?*

Like a boat being slowly drawn toward the center of a swirling maelstrom, Raptor couldn't control his thoughts or derail them off the painful track they were currently traveling. *Just like the incredible odds of Jesus fulfilling the Old Testament prophecies of the coming Messiah. If you can't deny Steven's two signs and his prophecy, then how can you deny over three hundred prophecies that Jesus fulfilled?*

There has to be another explanation, Raptor argued with himself. *Those prophecies MUST have been written after the fact.* Even though he knew the statement was untrue, he clung to it stubbornly like one clings to the seat of a sinking ship.

You know that the first part of Steven's prophecy is correct, even though he had no way of knowing your past. And the middle section certainly appears to be coming true. But if you accept some of it, then that means that ALL of it is likely true. Even the end...

Thirty-one days.

Although Tartarus had no moon, stars, or seasons with which to measure time, the founders kept with the original calendar from earth, marking the passing of the days by brightening their man-made lights in the daytime and dimming them in the evening. Steven had given the prophecy on the eleventh of January, and it was now early in the morning of February second. *Including today, that leaves only nine more days.*

Disturbed, Raptor looked over at the dim light from the lamp on the nearby desk. As someone who had been awakened suddenly in the middle of the night and forced to fight for his life, he had learned long ago to sleep with at least a weak light source still burning. Now, he stared at the lamp as if its soft illumination might somehow bring his thoughts into alignment. *How is it possible to hold two contradictory beliefs simultaneously? I've seen and experienced too many things that make me believe there is no God, but I've also seen and experienced too many things that make me believe there is a God.*

But what if he is real? How could anyone even know which religion, if any, has the truth? Frustrated by confusion, his logical mind once more sought out a lifeline and latched upon the conversation he'd had with Braedon before leaving Elysium.

"Each worldview attempts to answer four basic questions. First, where did we come from? Origin. Second, why is there pain and suffering? Evil. Third, what's the purpose of life? Meaning. And fourth, what's going to happen to us when we die? Destiny."

Since meeting Braedon for the first time, all the questions Raptor had buried deep in his psyche had somehow boiled up to the surface and demanded his attention. He had used Braedon's four questions to consider his own atheistic beliefs and wasn't comfortable with the answers. But back in Dehali, when he had asked the same questions of Hinduism and Buddhism, he hadn't been satisfied with those answers either. Nothing seemed to gratify his logical mind or resonate with the emptiness he felt in his soul.

Zahra had added fuel to the fire by reminding him of his Islamic roots. *I wonder how Islam would answer these questions?* He pondered the thought for a moment before he realized that, unlike Hinduism and Buddhism, he wouldn't have to talk to others to find those answers. The training from his childhood provided all of the information he needed.

Where did we come from? Allah created the universe. Why is there pain and suffering? Because of the sin of people and in order for Allah to test us. What's the purpose of life? To worship Allah and follow his commands, particularly the Five Pillars. What's going to happen to us when we die? We face judgment. Believers go to paradise, unbelievers to punishment.

Raptor paused his current trail of thought. *No, that's not entirely true. Belief alone won't do it.* Although he knew some imams stressed belief in Allah for salvation, he remembered clearly the words of the Qur'an: *Then those whose balance (of good deeds) is heavy, they will be successful. But those whose balance is light, will be those who have lost their souls; in hell will they abide.*[1]

Even as the words passed through his mind, a new thought struck him, causing a wave of fear and anxiety to grip him. *No matter what turns out to be true, death isn't looking like it's going to be any fun for you, Rahib. If you compare your 'good' deeds with your 'bad' deeds, your 'bad' deeds would win by a landslide! You'd better hope there isn't a God, because then you'd simply cease to exist. But if Hinduism or Buddhism is true, you'll be reincarnated and suffer for the negative karma you've built up. If Islam is true, then you'll go to hell because your 'balance is light' and because you didn't follow the Five Pillars. And if Christianity is true...*

The last thought turned his stomach. He had known only a handful of sincere Christians in his life, including Steven, Braedon, and Kianna. Although he respected each of them for their skills, he still refused to entertain the idea that their beliefs could be true. *Then again, how much do you really know about what they believe? Have you ever given it serious consideration, or just dismissed it completely because of what happened nineteen years ago?*

Raptor sat up in the bed, the physical movement serving to dampen the emotional turmoil in his soul. *No! Christianity can't be real either. There's too much pain and suffering in this world. If God truly is 'loving' and 'merciful,' then why would he allow people—especially those who follow him—to suffer so much? What kind of God would let Steven be disgraced and allow his family to turn away from him? What kind of God would let Braedon's wife be taken and sold as a slave? And if that's the kind of God he is, then I don't want to serve him even if he is real. He doesn't even love his own people!*

A muffled cry coming from the adjoining room broke into Raptor's thoughts. His instincts immediately kicked in. Within seconds he had grabbed his pistol, which he always kept near his head when he slept, and was standing to the left of the door connecting the rooms, his senses alert. A moment later, Jade was in position along the wall on the right side of the door, all traces of sleep having evaporated. Coming up behind him, a groggy Charon shot a questioning look at Raptor.

The three of them were frozen in silence as they listened intently to what were clearly the sounds of someone in distress. Muffled sobs were punctuated by pleas for mercy. Jade's eyes flickered knowingly toward where Xavier was sleeping on one of the beds, then toward where Kianna slept on the floor. Catching her meaning, Raptor shook his head in reply, indicating that there was no time to wake the others. With his pistol gripped firmly in one hand, he moved his other hand so that it hovered over the door's activation switch. Just as he was about to press it, he heard a soft voice filter through the wall, the words gentle and soothing.

"Cat, it's okay. I'm here. It was just a bad dream."

Jade, Charon, and Raptor instantly relaxed as they exchanged relieved glances with each other. Frustrated at having his sleep interrupted by a false alarm, Charon quickly plopped back down on the bed on which he had been sleeping. Raptor and Jade, their heartbeats slowly reverting to normal, began to turn away from the door when they heard Braedon begin speaking again, the emotion and love in his voice rooting them to their spots.

"Dear Lord," he prayed, "please comfort my hurting wife. You know the grief and trauma she has suffered. Please, God, let your Holy Spirit fill her and be a balm to her wounded soul..." His voice cracked as his own sorrow choked off his words. "Jesus, please...turn her mourning into dancing. Help her to rest in your loving arms. Take away all traces of this nightmare, and give her your peace that passes all human understanding. Remove this burden from her. Reveal yourself to my beautiful bride, and help her to know you as the loving father that you are."

The sounds of Catrina's sobbing slowly faded away, leaving a profound stillness in the room. After several moments of silence, Raptor felt his senses return to normal, as if he had just awakened from some magical spell. Locking eyes with Jade, he saw the same expression mirrored in her face. Uncomfortable at having eavesdropped on such a profound moment of tenderness between husband and wife, Raptor and Jade returned wordlessly to where they had been sleeping.

As Raptor lay down on the bed next to the sleeping form of Xavier, he was suddenly overcome by a deep sense of longing that welled up within him. He had felt this emptiness resurrect itself many times before, but never had it been this consuming. Frustrated at himself for what he saw as a moment of weakness, he pushed against it by chiding himself. *Rahib, you fool. Don't be getting all sentimental now.*

However, as he tried to return to sleep, he simply couldn't shake off the emotion and power of Braedon's prayer. As he drifted off to sleep, he found himself wondering what it would be like to have his own wounds healed, his own burdens removed, his own nightmares taken away...and to know real peace for once in his life.

1. Surah 23:102-103.

12

NIGHTTIME VISITORS

As the burning brilliance of the Golden Dome faded into the gentle glow of the sleep cycle, so too did the chaotic sounds of a city recovering from tragedy fade. Blaring emergency sirens became less frequent, raging fires were doused into smoldering embers, and the wails of the trapped and dying were replaced by the soft groans of the wounded and grieving.

Completely masked by the background ambiance of the debilitated city, the access hatch to the city sewers slid open. A moment later, a vaguely human-shaped haze emerged from the opening and flitted quickly across the deserted street where it seemed to merge with the stone wall protecting the beautiful home. However, after several seconds, the haze reappeared as it moved silently up and over the ten-foot wall.

Once in the shadowy yard, nearly all semblance of human form vanished in the dim light. The only indication that anything was moving toward the house was the occasional odd ripple in the air. The ripple didn't stop when it reached the building, but rather climbed up the wall, like the small movement of earth that accompanied an animal as it burrowed just below the surface of the ground.

It finally came to a halt as it reached one of the second-story windows. Nearly half a minute passed before the security on the window was deactivated and the window opened, allowing the nearly invisible shadow to enter.

Across the street, three figures climbed up through the sewer hatch, each one larger than the previous one. They ran toward the now open gate, slipped through it, and closed it behind them. Within moments, they were standing inside the entrance of the home.

As the three figures watched, a shadow detached itself from the wall and coalesced into the form of a human dressed completely in black, including a helmet with a dark, V-shaped visor that covered the man's entire head. *I have done as you requested, Prometheus. The woman's husband and children have been sedated. There will be no interruptions.*

The giant, seven-foot-tall, genetically and technologically enhanced Guardian leader nodded in confirmation. *Good work, Specter,* he replied through the TeleConnect channel. Turning toward the figure on his right, who was an exact duplicate of Specter in both uniform and size, Prometheus opened a different TC channel. *Virus, are we still in the dark?*

The helmeted head shook slightly. *Yes. There have been no spikes in the military TC channels since I momentarily jammed the cameras feeds on this street.*

Good. Continue monitoring. Cerberus, stay here and keep your senses alert for any sign of unusual activity outside.

The Hybrid standing on his leader's left side turned immediately toward the front door, his elongated snout sniffing the air. Using the heightened senses of smell and hearing from the canine part of his DNA, he took up his guard post just inside the front door, his gaze focused intently on the street.

Specter, come with me. Confident in the abilities of his fellow Guardians, Prometheus moved through the house and climbed the stairs toward the second floor, followed closely by Specter. Stepping into the master bedroom, he approached the sleeping couple that lay completely oblivious of their unwelcome visitors.

Reaching out a gloved hand, Prometheus poked the soft flesh of the woman's arm, causing her to stir. "Zahra Ahmed, it's time to wake up."

As the sound of the deep, gravely voice penetrated the fog of sleep, Zahra slowly opened her eyes. However, the instant the first terrifying image of the Guardian seeped into her lethargic brain, a sudden surge of adrenaline and fear chased away all traces of sleep. Letting out an ear-splitting scream, she sat up in the bed and pressed her back against the headboard as if hoping her efforts might somehow allow her to pass through it and the wall to escape from the dark visage.

Having anticipated the woman's reaction, Prometheus had turned off his enhanced hearing momentarily. The Titan had once struggled to come to terms with his fear-inducing appearance. He knew that everyone he encountered thought of him as a monster. It had taken him many years and a bout with depression that nearly ended in suicide before he came to grips with the reality that that was exactly what he was and was intended to be. The scientists that created him made sure to give him the scaly hide and twin horns of the vicious, reptilian *svith*, but with the body structure of a human. But where once he had loathed the horror he saw reflected in the eyes of others, he now relished the feeling of power it gave him.

A wicked grin spread across his face as he watched the helpless woman attempt to rouse her comatose husband. His twisted pleasure only increased as her failed attempts to wake him heightened her already nearly overwhelming panic. Staring back at the intruder, Zahra appeared to shrink as she huddled close to her husband.

Growing tired of the predictable entertainment, Prometheus decided to get down to business. "Zahra Ahmed, I won't hurt you or your family if you cooperate. I need some information." Slowly, the Guardian's words worked their way through Zahra's paralyzed mind. "I...Who...who are you? Are you...are you a *djinn*?"

Prometheus let out a throaty laugh. "Really? Do I look like I'm made of smokeless flame? Then again, I suppose I do probably look like some of the more fanciful artist renditions of your rebellious devils. But, no, I'm not one of your mythological, invisible spirit creatures, and I'm certainly no legendary genie in some magic lamp. I'm a purely manmade monstrosity.

"I'm here because I'm looking for your brother, Rahib. Where is he?"

Zahra frowned in confusion and shock. "Rahib? But...but why...?" Suddenly, she inhaled sharply as the truth struck her, followed by a fresh wave of fear. "You...you're the Guardians from Elysium!"

Prometheus narrowed his eyes. "Ye-e-es," he said, drawing out the word. "I take it by your reaction that your brother mentioned us."

"No...I...everyone in Bab al-Jihad has heard of you," Zahra muttered.

"You are a terrible liar," the Titan said with a sneer as his computer-enhanced brain quickly recorded and analyzed her pulse, blood pressure, and other vital signs. "Even without your pathetic attempt to suppress your emotions, it's clear you're lying because you realized who I was immediately after I mentioned your brother's name. So let's stop playing this little 'game' and focus on what's important. Where is he?"

Zahra paled. "I...I honestly don't know! He didn't tell me. In fact, he specifically *didn't* tell me because he said that I couldn't be forced to tell others if I didn't know myself!"

"Then why was he here?"

"He just...wanted to make sure my family and I were unharmed after the earthquake."

Unable to find any trace of falsehood, Prometheus frowned. "How are you supposed to contact him, then?"

"I can't contact him," she said, beginning to tremble once again under the pressure of the Guardian's questions. "He said he would contact me. Please, you must believe me!"

Although he knew that she was telling the truth, Prometheus became frustrated at what was beginning to look like a dead end in his search. Taking a step forward, he gripped her delicate chin in his monstrous claw. "Don't play with me, woman! I *will* get the information I want!" Letting go of her, he motioned toward Specter, who had remained motionless in the doorway during the entire confrontation. Immediately, the other Guardian spun around and left the room.

"Please!" Zahra cried, her voice becoming hoarse and weak. "I don't know where he is!"

"Then help me find him!" Prometheus growled. "Your father must have some way."

Before his victim could respond, Specter returned carrying a limp form. At the sight of her daughter, Zahra screamed once more, her breathing coming through choked gasps. "No! Please! I've told you all I know! Don't hurt her!"

"You're lying!" Prometheus howled, sending flecks of spittle toward his prisoner. "I see it in your eyes! You know something!"

Zahra collapsed onto the bed and covered her face as she wept. Further irritated by the woman's lack of cooperation, Prometheus felt his frustration give way to anger. "Specter, cut her!"

"NO! Wait!" Zahra pleaded. Moving onto her hands and knees, she reached a shaking hand toward her interrogator. For several seconds she remained in that position, until finally, ultimately defeated, she lowered her arm and bowed her head. When she spoke, her voice was muffled and barely audible. "I will tell you what you want to know…just, please, don't hurt my daughter."

Specter remained unmoving with the young girl in his arms as Prometheus leaned toward Zahra. "How do I find him?"

"I gave him a gift that has a tracking chip in it."

"How fortunate for you. What is the chip's code?"

"F473-X49B."

Prometheus mentally entered the code into his implanted computer. A second later, the location was confirmed. Grinning wickedly, Prometheus held up the index finger on his right hand. A small needle extended from the hidden sheath beneath the skin of his fingertip. "Thank you, Zahra Ahmed. You have been most helpful."

Zahra's eyes grew wide as the giant leaned toward her and jabbed the needle into her arm. For several seconds, her body convulsed slightly as the foreign liquid pumped through the needle invaded her nervous system. Then, with a final gasp, she wilted onto the bed, her eyes closed and her body motionless.

Turning away, Prometheus headed toward the door of the room, his mind already focusing on what lay ahead. A minute later, he and the other three Guardians had left the house and melted away into the shadows of the city to continue their hunt.

13

THE MAP

Braedon awakened the next morning to a soft rapping on the door that separated the rooms. A moment later, he heard Kianna's voice coming through the wall. "Braedon, Catrina, are you awake?"

"Yeah," he answered, sliding his arm out from underneath his wife, the movement causing her to stir . "Give us just a minute." Sitting up, he felt a painful stiffness in his muscles. On three different occasions throughout the night, Catrina had jolted awake from nightmares. Each time, it had taken him between twenty and forty minutes to calm her enough for her to fall back asleep. He quickly found that simply stroking her hair worked best. However, both times he did it, he fell asleep in an awkward position that left him with a kink in his neck and a sore lower back.

Sliding off the bed, he stepped toward the adjoining door. Although the others had given them their privacy, both he and Catrina had slept in their clothes, uncertain as to how long the precious time together would last. Touching the control on the wall, he opened the door.

"I'm sorry to bother you, but...Raptor's getting ready to go somewhere," Kianna said in a whisper. "He didn't say where's

THE TARTARUS CHRONICLES BOOK 3: BAB AL-JIHAD

he's going, but he's taking Jade with him and leaving Charon here. I thought you might want to know."

Glancing over Kianna's shoulder and into the other room, Braedon saw that Jade was in the process of putting on her *burqa* while Raptor was checking the power setting on his blaster pistol. To the left, Xavier was checking out the news-feeds while Charon was devouring a large plate of *kokli* eggs and *griblin* sausage.

Stepping past Kianna into the room, Braedon ran his fingers through his short-cropped hair as he quickly checked the time on his implanted chronometer. "What's going on?"

Without pausing or looking over, Raptor placed the weapon in the holster just inside the left breast of his *svith*-scale jacket. Reaching over to a nearby table, he grabbed the backpack resting there and began examining its contents as he replied. "Jade and I are going out to do a little…shopping. I need the rest of you to stay here, if you think you can manage that."

The man's sarcasm triggered Braedon, enhanced by his lack of sleep and sore body. "So, you're leaving Charon here to babysit us this time, is that it? Do you really think he's going to be able to stop me if I want to leave?"

Surprised by the uncharacteristic challenge, Raptor turned to look at him even as Charon jumped to his feet, the plate of food momentarily forgotten.

"You really think you can take me down, pretty boy?" Charon snapped as he flexed his large muscles.

A cutting response flew to Braedon's lips. However, they died there a moment later as his ears picked up the sound of his wife's breathing quicken, signaling the onset of another possible panic attack. As if cold water had just been tossed into his face, Braedon held up his hands in surrender. "I apologize, Charon. My comment was out of line. I didn't mean to provoke you."

Caught off guard by the sudden change, Charon hesitated, then offered a lame, face-saving threat. "Yeah, that's right. You'd better back down, soldier boy. If you mess with me, no amount of fancy karate moves will save you."

With his mind more clearly focused, Braedon started over. "Raptor, I understand that we might be a liability to you because we don't speak Arabic, but are you at least going to fill us in on the plan? Have you figured out where Gunther and Travis are being held and how we're going to rescue them?"

Zipping up the backpack, Raptor sighed. "Fine. You want the plan? Here it is. I'm still trying to get the final pieces in place, but I can tell you that Gunther and Travis are being held in the building behind the Golden Dome on the island in the center of the city. I've got a connection that'll help us get into the complex undetected. If I remember correctly, Gunther said that once he got the readings from the Dehali portal, it wouldn't take him long to calibrate the Vortex weapon. However, he also said he'd need to access an already open portal in order to reverse it, and the only one in the city is inside that same complex.

"So, we have two options: we can take the Vortex weapon with us on the rescue mission and hope to somehow rescue the scientists, give them time to calibrate it, get to the Bab al-Jihad portal, and use the Vortex to reverse it—all without raising an alarm—or we can find another portal somewhere nearby."

"Okay, so we leave the weapon behind and focus on freeing Gunther and Travis, then find another portal," Xavier said, joining the conversation. As he continued, Braedon felt Catrina come to stand next to him. "Piece of cake. So, what's the problem?"

Raptor frowned at the con man. "The problem is that by rescuing the others, we're bound to stir up a hornet's nest. I don't think we'd make it very far from the city on the main roads before we are caught. I think our best bet is to find another portal closer by, preferably somewhere they wouldn't expect us to go." Although he would never admit it to the others, in the back of his mind, Raptor recognized that his ulterior motive behind his decision was the rapidly approaching deadline in Steven's prophecy.

"But we can't return to Dehali," Kianna said. "That means the next closest portal is in New China—over five days away!"

"Not exactly," Raptor replied. "There's another one: in the Labyrinth."

"The Labyrinth!" Xavier echoed incredulously, followed a moment later by a nervous laugh. "That's pretty funny, Raptor. I mean, you really had me believing for a second that you were serious."

"I am serious."

The smile faded instantly from Xavier's face. "But...but the Labyrinth is...I mean, everyone's heard the stories: endless tunnels that don't just go in four directions, but up and down as well; strange creatures that drop on you from above or drag you down a deep hole; large, horned monsters that hunt in the pitch-black darkness. The unfortunate souls that enter through the portal by the Well never make it out alive."

"Those stories are exaggerated to scare little girls," Charon jibed, casting Xavier a sideways grin. "Raptor and I have heard that not only have people gone deep into the Labyrinth, they've also mapped it out."

Raptor nodded. "If we go in with the right weapons and scanning devices, we can avoid most trouble and scare off anything that comes at us. Which brings me back to the present: Jade and I are going to do a little snooping around to see if we can find someone who has a map."

"I know someone."

The group turned in unison toward the source of the soft voice that came from behind Braedon. "W-what?" Braedon stammered as he looked at his wife in shock.

The sudden attention from the others caused Catrina to shrink back behind her husband, using him as a shield. "I...I know someone who has a map. My husb—Zarrar had many friends in the military. One of those friends was assigned to a team who was tasked with mapping out the Labyrinth. They went in frequently to capture some of the creatures that live there."

Charon harrumphed. "So what? A lot of good it does us now. You all killed her husband and the whole city is looking for you. Even if this guy has a map, there's no way we could get it."

"Yes, there is," Catrina spoke up louder this time. "I know his wife very well, and I trust her. All I have to do is meet with her and ask her to get it for me."

"Can't you just contact her?" Xavier chimed in. "You know—use the TeleConnect."

Catrina shook her head. "She doesn't have an implant. I guess I could try a direct connection."

"No," Braedon stated emphatically. "That could be traced. It sounds too risky. If you're recognized..."

"But I always wear a *burqa*," Catrina interjected. "Tabinda and her husband own and operate a weapons shop. I've been there many times with Zarrar. I know my way around. We would appear to be nothing more than another set of customers."

Although Braedon was clearly opposed to the idea, the others were starting to view it as a definite possibility. Glancing around the room, Braedon could see the eyes of Jade, Raptor, Charon, and Xavier lose their focus, indicating that they were having a silent conversation through their implants. Looking down at Catrina in concern, Braedon whispered to her. "Cat, this is too soon. I don't think you should do this. What if..."

Catrina smiled weakly at him. "I need to do this, Braedon. If I can help in any way, I want to do so. Please."

Stepping closer, Kianna looked intently at the other woman. "Are you absolutely certain you can trust Tabinda with your life?"

"Yes, I am," she replied with confidence.

Having finished their implant conversation, Raptor and the others turned to look at Catrina once more. "Fine. We'll try Catrina's friend. But we'll do it our way."

Raptor, let me just state once more—for the record—that I'm getting tired of sitting on the sidelines and playing lookout while you get to have all the fun! Charon stated through the TC channel.

Don't worry. I'll make sure you get to risk your life and freedom next time, Raptor replied. *For what it's worth, I'd rather have you by my side than Braedon. But there's no way he would've let Catrina go with me unless he was there.*

Yeah, yeah, and Jade gets to go to back up Catrina if the women get separated, and you need Xavier for distraction. I understand the logic, I just don't like it.

And don't forget, my friend, that your bulk and size are intimidating to most people. We wouldn't want your legion of fans noticing you and blowing our cover, Raptor replied with a slight grin that was mostly covered by his fake beard and mustache.

Ha, Charon replied mirthlessly. *What's the point of a disguise if I don't get to try it out?*

Believe me, there'll be plenty for you to do before this is over, I can guarantee that. Besides, you've got Kianna to keep you company. Speaking of which, has she been able to hack into the street cameras yet?

Yeah. She's ready to cut the feeds on your signal.

Good. We're approaching the store now. How does every-thing look from your angle?

There was a slight pause before Charon replied. *It looks like any other day of shopping for the happy citizens of Bab al-Ji-had, except, of course, for those two goons in their souped-up armored suits at each end of the street. They're scanning the marketplace very carefully. They've probably got their facial-recognition programs running. Maybe we'll get lucky and one of them will recognize Xavier as he's strolling along and rid us of his irritating humor.*

Keep dreaming. He's too good for that. Did he deliver his package?

Yeah, about a minute ago. He's milling about and working his way back to the Spelunker.

Okay. Just be ready. Jade and I are moving into position now. With that, Raptor closed down the connection and focused on his acting. Signaling to Jade, who appeared to be examining a necklace from one of the nearby street vendors, he motioned for her to join him. Responding immediately, she adjusted her black *burqa*, then closed the distance between them and followed him as he entered the store.

Once inside, Raptor casually assessed the situation. There were eight other people inside the medium-sized building in addition to the two men running the main counter that took up a majority of the east wall. Although most of the guns and other weapons were hanging on racks behind the counter and on display in glass cases, there were several aisles of accessories, carry bags, and an assortment of other supplies. As expected, the recent earthquake and tension in the city had increased the business of weapons sales. Although this meant there were more people in the store than normal, Raptor had been doing this kind of undercover work to know that he could use it to his advantage.

Striding purposefully up to the main counter, he took one of the numbered discs from the dispenser. Activating his Tele-Connect, he sent a brief message to Braedon, then pretended to examine several of the items on a nearby shelf while he waited. A few moments later, the door behind them opened as Braedon and Catrina entered the shop.

As the couple headed toward the main counter to collect their own numbered disc, Raptor watched them out of the corner of his eye as he pretended to browse the merchandise. However, as he saw them step up to the counter and take a number, a sense of unease settled in the pit of his stomach.

I told you I didn't think she was ready for this, Jade said through their implant connection, her keen eye picking out the same telltale mistakes that could spell trouble for the operation. *If she keeps looking around like a caged animal, she's going to rouse suspicion. Not only that, but I've seen her put her hand on her stomach at least twice. She swallows her stress until it makes her sick. I've seen it before.*

She seemed pretty determined to do this, Raptor replied. *Sometimes the waiting is the worst part. Once things get moving, she might be okay. And if not, we go to plan B.*

Jade snickered beneath her *burqa.* Although he couldn't see her face through the black wire mesh, he could easily imagine based on firsthand experience the eye roll and accompanying irritated expression on her face. *Running toward the Spelunker like a herd of stampeding three-toed rock jumpers is not what I would call a plan.*

Raptor fought to suppress his smile. *I never thought I'd live to see the day when you'd use one of Xavier's colorful expressions. And for the record, it is* too *a plan when you have half your team in disguise and the other half armed and holding down the escape route.*

Yeah, well I'd feel a lot better if I had a blaster in my hand.

It's a good thing we didn't bring them, though. Charon was right about the detectors. Besides—wait a second. Braedon's contacting me.

After switching the channel of his implant to briefly hear the other's message, Raptor returned to his silent conversation with Jade. *He says that Catrina has confirmed that Tabinda is in back. She has asked to speak with her. Here we go.*

A moment later, Raptor saw a woman come through a door behind the main counter and walk over to where Catrina waited.

Charon, have Kianna cut the camera feeds. Xavier, light 'em up.

A few seconds later, the entire store shook, causing several of the customers to fall to the floor as two explosions erupted out in the market.

14

CLOSE CALL

The two men behind the counter had semiautomatic laser rifles in their hands before the first vibrations from the explosion had fully passed through the store. The older of the two turned toward Tabinda and barked out an order for her to stay down behind the counter as the other man pushed past the startled customers toward the front entrance.

Although she knew the explosion was coming, Catrina still found herself reeling from the stab of panic that shot through her. Dropping to the ground, she fought against her rising terror. Staring around in confusion, she watched as Braedon and Raptor, both following their predetermined script, ran for the door and windows along with the rest of the men to see what was going on out in the street. As the men began shouting and pointing out the window, several of them opened the door of the store and went out into the street. Unable to contain himself any longer, the man who had stayed behind the counter finally left his post to join the rest, his rifle still held close to his chest.

Dazed, Catrina heard only snippets of conversation coming from the group.

"—bomb—"

"—mech suits damaged—"

"—terrorists in the city—"

"Snap out of it!" Jade said in a forced whisper as she crouched down next to Catrina. "Xavier and the others have done their job, now it's time to do ours." Seeing the confused expression on her pale face, the Asian woman dug her fingers into Catrina's shoulder.

Letting out a short gasp of pain, Catrina pulled back from the black-clad figure before finally realizing who she was. "Jade, I...I'm sorry." Glancing nervously toward the entrance, she finally returned her gaze to the woman she had come to see. "Tabinda, it's me, Sabihah," she said, switching from English to Arabic as she quickly turned up the top portion of her *burqa* to reveal her face to the other.

Unlike her visitors, whose features were fully obscured by the wire mesh of the *burqa*, Tabinda only wore a dark-blue-and-gold *niqab*. Although the thick scarf covered her entire head and face, it left her eyes visible. And in those eyes, Catrina saw both shock and fear reflected in her gaze.

"Sabihah? But...but your husband was...killed! Everyone is looking for you!" Suddenly remembering the presence of the stranger, Tabinda's eyes darted toward Jade.

"It's okay," Catrina said as she laid a calming hand on Tabinda's arm. "She's a friend. She helped me escape from Zarrar's cruelty."

Tabinda's wariness lessened only slightly at the other woman's reassurance. "Why are you here? If Nisar or his brother catches you, they will turn you in! You have to leave now! They have cameras everywhere!"

Catrina's hand moved absentmindedly toward her abdomen as Tabinda's worry caused her own anxiety to spike. It was only Jade's forceful presence beside her that allowed her to maintain her focus. Taking a deep breath, she plunged ahead. "Don't worry. We have a friend who disabled the cameras before we entered."

Although Catrina's reassurance took the edge off the other woman's concern, Tabinda still appeared skittish.

"We can't leave. Not yet," Catrina continued. "We need your help. We don't have a lot of time. We need a copy of the map from the Labyrinth. Do you have one?"

Tabinda's eyes grew even wider as she stared in shock. "The... the Labyrinth? Why would you want that? You can't possibly—"

"I don't have time to explain," Catrina said as she cast a furtive look over her shoulder. "Please. I'm trusting you with my life! If you ever considered me a friend, please do this for me!"

Throwing her own look toward where her husband was stationed just outside the door, she nodded toward Catrina, then climbed slowly to her feet. All the while keeping an eye on the group of men, she crouched and moved slowly along the length of the counter.

Annoyed by the frightened woman's slow movements, Jade let out a hissing curse. Drawing closer to Catrina, Jade continued to pretend that they were huddled together out of fear, when in reality she was hoping her proximity would both keep Catrina focused and shield her fear from any onlookers.

Finally, after what seemed like an eternity, Tabinda reached a small, locked cabinet that was mounted along the wall at the same height as the counter. Still keeping her eyes on her husband, she slowly reached up and punched in the access code. With nervous sweat dripping into her eyes, Tabinda inched her shaking hand into the cabinet.

Time seemed to slow to a crawl for Catrina. With each tick of the clock came an increase in her anxiety. And with the increased anxiety came the twisting pain in her gut. The churning, unsettling sensation triggered within her memories of the past...memories of the numerous times when she had waited in dreaded anticipation of the outburst and torment she knew would be unleashed upon her by her "husband" for some minor infraction.

As the memories replayed in her mind, she doubled over and began to cough, the muscles in her chest constricting from the emotional stress. "Catrina," she heard her name whispered from nearby, "you're going to get us all killed! You've got to pull yourself together!"

Despite her best efforts, Catrina winced as Jade's words caused a new wave of panic to stab at her stomach. Her breathing became shallower as her lungs began to constrict. She glanced nervously back and forth between Tabinda and the entrance to the store.

Reacting to the woman's growing hysteria, Jade placed herself between Catrina and the men gathered at the entrance. As she moved, she sent a quick warning to Braedon and Raptor via her implant before returning her attention to her companion. Fighting the growing urge to slap some sense into the woman, Jade gripped Catrina's shoulders and forced calmness into her voice before speaking. "Breathe. You need to calm down!"

Although Jade was now blocking Catrina's view of the gathered men, she continued to stare in their direction, their excited voices still fueling her anxiety. Once again, Jade dug her fingers into the other woman's shoulders, the physical pain momentarily overriding the panic. Crying out, Catrina's eyes snapped out of their staring spell and locked onto Jade's. "We...we have to... to leave," Catrina gasped. "If Nisar...if he catches us...he'll—"

Swearing under her breath in frustration, Jade brought her face close to Catrina's. "We're not leaving without that stupid map. Now shut up before—"

The sound of a man's voice yelling in her direction caused her to leave the last thought unfinished. Turning her veiled head around, she found that it was already too late. Catrina's episode hadn't gone unnoticed. The store owner, whom she guessed to be Nisar, had just reentered the store and was the source of the shouting.

Jade let out an irritated sigh. "So much for the easy way," she mumbled.

Even before the last words were out of her mouth, she watched as Braedon and Raptor sprang into action simultaneously. Being the nearest to Nisar, Raptor grabbed the rifle out of the surprised man's hands while Braedon leaned back, planted his foot into the man's torso, and pushed. Caught off guard, Nisar fell backward into the other men standing in the doorway, causing the whole group to fall out onto the street in a heap.

Kianna, NOW! Raptor called out through the TC. Immediately, the reinforced doors of the shop slammed close with a thud. With the group of men trapped outside, Raptor withdrew a small device from his pocket and placed it on the door.

The jammer is in place, Raptor said, filling the rest of the team in on the situation. *They won't be coming in through the front anytime soon.*

Unless they get one of the mech suits up and running, Xavier replied. *Several of the men you kicked out are already heading toward one of the city's military goons.*

I thought you took them out of commission, Raptor replied, his own frustration at their predicament reaching its boiling point. Leaving the front entrance, he sprinted over to join Braedon, Jade, and Catrina.

I did, but not for long. You wanted a distraction and I gave you one. But with my limited resources, and in order to make the bombs small enough to avoid detection, I had to use more flash and less substance. I merely fried their circuits. Do you have any idea how hard it was to get close enough to the mech suits to plant the bombs? Even with the disguise, it still took all of my considerable acting skills to—

How long until they reboot their systems? Raptor interrupted the other's ego-building monologue. Next to him, Braedon was helping Catrina to her feet. Reaching down, Raptor picked up the stolen rifle that the other had discarded when he went to help his wife.

You've got about a minute before they can reroute the power around the damaged circuits. Uh-oh. Hey, you'd better move fast. From what I can see through my sight-enhancers, there's a group of about six military vehicles headed this direction. We've got probably no more than three minutes before they arrive.

Raptor swore at the news. *Is Charon in place?*

Yep.

Good. Bring the Spelunker around. We'll meet you out back in sixty seconds. Good luck.

Shutting off the connection, Raptor was about to speak when he noticed Tabinda huddled on the floor behind the counter, the holoprojector in her hand.

"Sabihah…what…what's going on?" she stammered as she stared in fear at the two strange men, one of whom was armed.

Taking charge of the situation, Raptor stepped forward and responded to the woman in Arabic. "We appreciate your help," he said as he took the holoprojector from her. Switching over to English, he looked at Jade, his barely contained anger seeping out. "Nisar is heading around back. Tell Zei to do a flyby and—"

"Already done," she snapped back. "I told you she wasn't ready!"

"Yeah, but at least we got what we came for," he retorted, holding up the device for her to see before pocketing it. "And unless you want to be the next practice specimen for the local interrogator, I suggest you save your detailed criticism of my leadership style for later." With his pent-up anger at least partially assuaged, Raptor spun on his heel and stormed through the door that led to the back of the building. Biting back her own rage, Jade pushed past the others and followed after Raptor.

Once they were gone, Catrina fought back her fear long enough to choke out a few words of apology to Tabinda. "I'm... I'm so sorry. Did...did Nisar see you?"

Tabinda shook her head. "No. When you started to cough, I hid behind the counter just before he turned around."

Catrina let out a sigh of relief. "We didn't mean...to cause you...trouble."

Behind the *niqab*, Catrina saw the fear ebb from the woman's eyes. Tabinda's expression softened, then quickly became resolute. "If that's true, then you need to take this." Standing, she pressed a hidden latch, opening a concealed drawer. Reaching in, she withdrew a medium-sized rectangular box and shoved it into Catrina's hand. "The map isn't valuable enough. If you don't take something more expensive, Nisar won't believe that this was a simple robbery."

Nodding in understanding, Catrina grimaced as a fresh wave of fear washed over her at the thought of the danger she had just placed her friend in. Climbing to her feet, she embraced Tabinda. Then, with the help of her husband, she disappeared through the doorway toward the back exit, hoping desperately that her friend wouldn't have to pay the price for her failure.

15

PLAN B

The moment the door closed behind him, Nisar felt fear and rage course through his body. Activating his implant, he quickly contacted the Bab al-Jihad military command and gave them a brief assessment of the situation. Closing down the connection, he turned to the men around him.

Fortunately for Nisar, these were not ordinary civilian buyers. As a former member of the military, he had built his business by selling to those he had served with. Of the eight "customers" who had been in the store at the time of the heist, he knew six of them by name.

And, they were always armed.

"The thieves must be planning on escaping out the back. You four come with me. We'll take the north alley. Viqaas," Nisar said, looking at the man who had been working in the store with him, "you and the other four take the south alley. Quickly! We must stop these infidels!"

Immediately, Viqaas and his four companions bolted toward the south alley as they pulled their various laser pistols out of their concealed holsters. Spinning around, Nisar motioned for the rest of the men to follow him. Within moments, they were running full speed down the alley along the north wall of the store.

Suddenly, a large hovervan floated past the far end of the alley toward the back of the store. "It's them! We can't let them get away!" Letting out a feral cry of hatred, Nisar and the men ran even faster, spurred on by the sight of their prey. Reaching the end of the alley, Nisar hugged the wall and peered around the corner. Pure rage overwhelmed him as he saw the thieves dart from the back exit of the store and into the vehicle. However, just as he was about to charge toward his enemies, a sudden voice screamed through his implant connection. *Something is dropping gas canisters on us! Nisar, watch out! They are—*

Before Viqaas could say any more, Nisar heard a crackling sound behind him. To his utter surprise, one of the men standing to his left began convulsing as blue bolts of energy coursed through his body. Spinning around, his eyes grew wide in alarm as another blast of energy seemed to materialize out of nowhere and strike two more of the men. Raising his weapon, Nisar fired haphazardly down the alley in a desperate attempt to find the hidden attacker. Backing up rapidly, he was just about to dive around the corner and take his chances with the thieves near the vehicle when he and the last of his posse were hit by another blast of blue energy.

"I like it!" Charon said as he stood and pushed the shimmering invisibility cloak over his shoulder. Admiring his handiwork as he stepped quickly over the unconscious forms of the men, he rounded the corner and moved toward the van, the large, rifle-sized weapon in his hands still humming with energy.

"This Volt weapon Steven was nice enough to leave with us is quite handy," he said as he climbed into the Spelunker. "One shot took out two men at once, and it has almost no kickback. Combined with this cloak, those guys never had a chance." Casting a glance at Braedon, who sat next to Catrina in the back, he snickered. "Steven must have had some interesting 'friends' back in Elysium in order to have gotten his hands on this tech."

Thankful that Braedon chose to ignore the comment, Raptor, who was seated in the middle section of the vehicle, turned his attention to the occupant of the front passenger seat. "Jade, what are you getting from Zei's camera feeds?"

"The gas she dropped on the men in the south alley did the trick. As far as the 'cavalry's' concerned, they're closing in. But if we head to the north, then loop back around, we should be able to get away before they close the noose around us."

"You heard her, Xavier. Get us out of here."

"You got it, boss," the con man said with a grin as he hit the accelerator and turned the vehicle onto the northbound street. Within a matter of minutes, the Spelunker and its occupants had left the area. Once the immediate threat of pursuit was gone, Xavier drove the vehicle down a few more streets before finding their prearranged stop. Pulling into the secluded back area of a nearby business, he brought the hovervan to a halt.

Immediately, all but Kianna, Braedon, and Catrina exited. Jade quickly sent Zei back into the air to scout the area. After just a few moments of scanning the images received from the miniature mammal's camera feeds, Jade gave the others the all clear. In just under a minute, the three men had removed all of the extra markings and decals that they had applied to the vehicle to disguise it, including the fake damage that Xavier had added to the rear window and bumper. As soon as the job was finished, they climbed back into the vehicle and resumed their trip to the hotel.

"Ah. It gives one a certain sense of satisfaction when a plan comes together, doesn't it?"

Jade snickered at Xavier's quip and threw a sidelong glare at Raptor.

"Somehow, I get the impression that Jade doesn't share your enthusiasm." Although Raptor's reply was to Xavier's comment, he looked toward the Chinese woman sitting in the front passenger seat. "However, as your leader, I for one appreciate it when one of my team members recognizes a good plan when they see one."

"Hah," Jade said, unable to hold in her irritation any longer. "If your plan A had been better, we wouldn't have had to resort to a plan B."

"Yeah, well, sometimes you have to just do your best with what you're given to work with. But, we got what we came for," he said, holding up the holographic projector containing the map. "And not only that, we escaped unnoticed, no one got hurt, and we even got a bonus surprise!"

"What bonus?" Charon asked with cautious curiosity, unsure of whether or not the surprise would be a good thing.

"I'm not actually sure. Let's ask the happy couple in back what they've got in that box."

Catrina, who had been completely wrapped up in her own self-punishing thoughts, suddenly roused at Raptor's words. Beside her, Braedon reached for the box still clenched tightly in her hands. As she handed it to him, he explained to the rest how they had received it from Tabinda.

Charon's expression lifted. "Well, quit keeping us in suspense! Let's see what's in it," he said as he reached over the back of the seat and grabbed the box from Braedon.

"Wait!"

The sudden cry from Xavier caused Charon to freeze with his hand on the box as if he was afraid it would explode. "What? What's wrong?" he said, his voice filled with a surge of concern.

Xavier activated the computer driver and spun around in his seat eagerly. At the sight of everyone's wide-eyed stares, he looked around in confusion. "What's wrong with you guys? Why are you all looking like a bunch of scared bol mice?"

"You just told Charon to wait, as if you thought it was a bomb or trap or something," Jade replied in exasperation. "What's that all about?"

"Oh," Xavier said, nonchalantly. "I just wanted you to wait until I had time to activate the computer driver. I don't wanna miss this."

The group let out a collective sigh and Jade punched Xavier in his arm, causing him to yelp in pain, an injured expression on his handsome features. As he massaged his arm, everyone else in the vehicle, with the exception of Catrina, leaned forward as the large man opened the box.

"Whew! Now here's a sweet bit of tech! This ought to make our whole job just a little easier, wouldn't you say, Raptor?" Charon said, his face beaming.

"Yes, I would," he replied, a grin of his own spilling onto his face.

"What is it?" Kianna asked, a bit alarmed. "Are those grenades?"

"In a sense," Braedon said. "But instead of exploding, these emit electromagnetic pulses. Nisar was probably stockpiling them to use against the Dehali war droids."

"Then what good will they be to us?"

Charon answered before Braedon could reply. "These little beauties can also be reconfigured to disrupt those big mech suits that the Bab al-Jihad military are so fond of," he said, holding up one of the small devices.

"This is definitely a positive development," Raptor said. "This might even change our plans and speed up our timetable." Opening up a TC channel, he sent a quick message to Jade and Charon. *Once we get back to the hotel, I want to talk to the two of you. Let's figure out how to use these to our best advantage. We also need to study the map and figure out the rest of our plan.*

The two offered a silent acknowledgement. Returning the EMP grenade to the box, Charon closed it. A few minutes later, they arrived back at the hotel. With their hopes higher than they had been in recent days, the group split up in order to reenter the hotel without attracting attention.

Raptor and Jade, who were the last to enter, sensed that something was wrong just as they stopped in front of the door of their room. Exchanging a quick glance of alarm, they reached for their concealed weapons. However, before either could extract their guns, the door opened and they felt an invisible force push them from behind, sending them sprawling into the darkened room.

Before they could get their bearings, large, clawed hands hauled them to their feet and bound their wrists painfully behind their back. Even with her hands tied, Jade tried to lash out at her captors. But just as she was preparing to kick, she felt a sharp pain in her arm. A moment later, she lay unconscious on the floor as the sedative she had just been given sapped her strength.

"Rahib Ahmed, I give you credit. You eluded me longer than most."

The iron grip of the hands that held him twisted him around to face the speaker, who stood near the far wall of the room. On the floor, Braedon, Charon, and the others lay unmoving. Lifting his eyes, he felt fear and panic race through his blood as he caught sight of his captors.

The Guardians had found them.

16

NO CHOICE

Raptor stared up at the twisted visage of the Guardian leader. He had seen Prometheus numerous times during his excursions to meet with Governor Mathison in Elysium, and he was well familiar with the Titan's reputation for cruelty and viciousness. That knowledge brought with it the certainty that the game was over. He and the others wouldn't live much longer, and if they did, their lives wouldn't be pleasant.

He had failed.

A faint smile edged its way across Prometheus's features as he observed the despair settle on his captive's shoulders and face. "I might thank you for giving me and my men a challenge, but this little chase has carried too high a price. Because of you and your scientist friend, I lost many talented and well-trained soldiers. True, I did gain some vital intel, mainly that your Dehali cohorts are planning to attack Elysium, and that they've developed a new device that can block implant communications, but our spies could have learned that soon enough.

"No. If we hadn't had to chase you and your friends halfway across Tartarus, my men would still be alive," Prometheus finished, an added tone of menace darkening his voice.

Summoning his courage and bravado, Raptor took a calming breath before replying. "Look, Prometheus, you've seen my work over the years and my loyalty to Mathison. Don't you even care why I split from him? I'm not a fool. I'm not going to turn my back on one of the most powerful men in all of Tartarus for nothing."

"There is little in this cursed underworld that I care about. Your squabble with Mathison is certainly not one of them."

"This isn't some stupid squabble!" Raptor shot back. As the passion in his voice increased, he tried to rise to his feet. However, the Hybrid Guardian standing behind him pushed him back down to his knees. Casting an irritated glance up at Cerberus, Raptor turned his gaze back to Prometheus. "You should care about this one if you want to live! In case you hadn't noticed, Tartarus hasn't been doing so well lately. It's being ripped apart! If that happens, you and everyone else in it are going to die!"

Prometheus stood as still as a statue, completely unfazed by Raptor's impassioned speech. "Yes, I've heard that rumor. Mathison's scientists believe that it's just a passing wave of seismic movement. We've had earthquakes before. This latest round, although more intense, will settle, as have all those in the past. Life in Tartarus will go on as it always has for the past two hundred years. You really should be careful what you choose to believe. In this case, your beliefs are going to have serious consequences."

It took Raptor several seconds to recover from the Titan's statement. Realizing that he'd hit a dead end, he tried a different tactic. "But there's more to it than that. Gunther and Travis have discovered how to reverse the portals and open a way back to earth! Isn't that worth something to you? Don't you want to escape the confines of this world?"

"You truly are pathetic, Rahib Ahmed. And desperate. Earth holds no interest for me and my men. We are products of this world. Our fate is bound to it. If earth is even real, we have no place in it."

Latching onto one last hope, Raptor tried again. "But the same device that can reverse the portals can also be used as a powerful weapon! You can't just leave that in the hands of Imam Ahmed. He could use it to destroy half your army in seconds!"

Prometheus laughed wickedly. "We know you have it in your possession. Nice try."

"But he *does* have Gunther and Travis, who know how to re-create it. He could have a working model in a month or less! He's preparing for war himself!"

"And who told you all this, your *sister,* Zahra?"

The tone of the Guardian leader's voice made Raptor's blood run cold. "How do you...what did you do to my sister?"

Prometheus smiled wickedly. "She's quite resilient. I honestly think she wouldn't have cracked if it had just been her. But with the lives of her children at stake, she didn't last very long."

A rage such as Raptor had never experienced before welled up inside him like lava in a boiling volcano. He moved so quickly that he caught even Cerberus off guard. Before the Hybrid could react, Raptor had leapt to his feet and lunged at Prometheus, his own safety completely forgotten. "You genetic freak! I swear I'll—"

Unlike his companion, Prometheus was fully prepared for the outburst. With one swift blow from the back of his massive hand, the Guardian knocked his captive to the floor, his twisted, reptilian features revealing his amusement. "Calm yourself, Rahib. I never dispose of an asset while it is still of use. And as long as you cooperate, your precious sister will remain unharmed, at least by me and my men."

Raptor nursed his lip that had been split open by Prometheus's blow. Still slightly dazed, he offered up no resistance as Cerberus picked him up from the floor.

"But we're wasting time," Prometheus continued. "A contingent of soldiers sent by your father is already on its way here to apprehend you."

Despite the seriousness of the Titan's statement, Raptor managed to regain some of his roguish composure. "Right. You've already threatened my sister to ensure my help. Don't you think throwing in this extra threat is a little over the top?"

Prometheus's expression lost its mirth. "It would definitely make things easier if only it were an idle threat. But I assure you, it is not. Virus, did you locate the tracking device?"

On the other side of the room, the technologically altered, Type-I Guardian retrieved the Qur'an Zahra had given Raptor. Despite his lack of faith, the sight of the unclean Cyborg touching the Islamic holy book sent an unbidden surge of discomfort through Raptor's body. "What are you doing with that?"

As Virus examined the back cover of the book, a sickening feeling settled in the pit of Raptor's stomach. Virus pulled back the corner of the book with his index finger and removed a small tracking chip.

"The imam knew you'd visit your sister, so he prepared a little gift for you," Prometheus said, indicating the Qur'an. "Your sister betrayed you."

Although his mind frantically sought out any rational theory to explain the existence of the tracker, he knew he couldn't escape the devastating truth: Zahra was working for his father.

"As you see, we have to leave this place right now," Prometheus said. "When my men have awakened your friends, you'll explain the situation to them and get them moving. You will then get into your vehicle and travel to the coordinates that Virus will send to you. Once there, I'll explain the rest of my terms. If you do not follow these instructions, you will die. We'll leave the tracker here in the room. That should give us some extra time before they discover that you've slipped out of their net."

Nodding to Virus, Prometheus turned and headed for the door of the room. Activating the invisibility cloak that he wore around his shoulders, he covered his head with it and exited. As Virus went around injecting a small stimulant into the others to rouse them, Cerberus left in the same fashion as his commander. Once his task was complete, Virus disappeared as well, leaving Raptor alone with his confused and dazed companions.

Without wasting a moment, Raptor explained the situation and mobilized his team. Moving with renewed urgency, the companions grabbed everything they could and headed out of the room in pairs as they had done previously. Finally, after several tense minutes, the team had once again assembled in the Spelunker, surprising and waking the sleeping *mindim*. Driving as casually as he could manage under the circumstances, Xavier piloted the vehicle down the road toward the coordinates given to them by the Guardians.

The apparent hopelessness of their current predicament put a damper on all conversation. After nearly twenty minutes of traveling in silence, Xavier finally announced that they had arrived.

The coordinates led to a small water filtration building near the northeast corner of the lake around which the city was built. All but one of the walls of the building had collapsed during the earthquake, and even that wall was leaning precariously.

"What in the...?" Xavier murmured. "I'm all for making a secret hideout in a broken-down, abandoned building, but this is even worse than any of the dumps you've led us to over the years, Raptor."

"Look on the bright side—at least we probably won't have to worry about anyone bothering us," he replied. "With the lake on one side and the small cliff wall separating us from the city proper, we're about as hidden as we can get."

"That could just mean that when that building collapses on top of us, it'll be a long time before anyone finds our bodies," Charon mumbled.

Once Xavier had brought the Spelunker to a halt near the cliff wall, the group exited the vehicle, their senses alert.

Moving up to stand next to Raptor's right shoulder, Charon studied their surroundings and sent his friend a short message via his implant. *This is a bad idea. We should make a run for it, or at least fight back.*

We'd never make it, Raptor replied. *The Guardians have us under surveillance. We wouldn't get far. And, they'd kill Zahra for sure. We have no choice but to play by their rules. Prometheus wants something from us, otherwise we'd already be dead or captured.*

Raptor ended the conversation as one of the human-sized Guardians materialized near the facility and motioned them to follow. He led Raptor and the others around the side of the one remaining wall to a stairway that was nearly covered with rubble. The group carefully worked their way around the debris and made it to a door at the bottom of the stairs. Their technologically altered guide opened it, and ushered them inside. With all of them gathered in the basement entrance, the black-clad Cyborg closed the door behind them, and the group found themselves facing the other three Guardians.

"Okay, Prometheus. You've got our attention. Now what is it you want from us?" Raptor asked without formalities.

The corner of the Guardian leader's lip curled. "I've come to offer you a deal."

Raptor's eyebrows rose in surprise and he cast a quick glance at Charon and Jade. "A deal? What kind of deal?"

"We'll help you rescue your friends from the imam's compound."

Again, it took Raptor several moments for his voice to work its way through his surprise. "And what could we possibly offer you in exchange for your help?"

Prometheus sneered. "You're going to contact your friends in the Dehali Military and get me one of the Implant Disruptor devices."

17

THE DEAL

Out of all of the phrases that Raptor guessed would come out of Prometheus's twisted mouth, a deal for Implant Disruptors didn't even make the top ten. In fact, the idea was so absurd and unexpected that Raptor nearly choked in surprise. Catching himself at the last moment, he remembered to play ignorant. "Implant Disruptors? I've never even heard of such a thing, unless you're referring to the Implant Inhibitors."

"Don't insult me or waste my time," Prometheus sneered. "My men and I have experienced firsthand just how false that statement is, and I know that you are aware of their existence."

Deciding it was useless to carry on the charade any longer, Raptor put on his best poker face. "Okay. Fine. Yeah, we know about them. Look, I appreciate your seeming confidence in my connections, but even you have to realize that there's no way the Dehali Military is going to part with a technology that gives them a clear edge over you and every other enemy. Even if you handed them Mathison himself on a silver platter I don't think they'd do it."

An amused grin made its way across the Guardian leader's features. "Interesting choice of words. Actually, that's almost exactly what I planned to offer."

Raptor and the others exchanged confused glances. "Come again?" Xavier quipped in unabashed shock. "Yes, I'm fully aware that General Ranjit would need something highly valuable in return for the disruptors. I'm not a fool. I don't expect you to convince him to turn them over just for aid in rescuing your friends," he remarked snidely. "So, I'm going to offer him a deal.

"You will contact him and have him send one of the devices here. Once it arrives, we will test it. If it checks out, we'll help you rescue your scientist friends. Once that's complete, my men and I will return to Elysium with the disruptor and use it to kill Governor Mathison."

The words stunned Raptor and the others. Charon was the first to find his voice. "But you *work* for Mathison. Why would you want to kill him? And why do you need a disruptor to do it?"

"Our reasons are unimportant to the deal."

Raptor eyed the part *svith*, part human as he struggled to wrap his brain around this new development. "Your motives are *definitely* important. What happens after Mathison's dead? Who takes over the government of Elysium? You? Ranjit's not going to want to replace one dictator with another one."

"I have no desire to rule," Prometheus replied. "In fact, we can offer General Ranjit even more. Once Mathison is out of the way, we'll destroy his research complex, along with the devices that he plans to use to control the populace through the implants."

"What you're offering sounds too good to be true," Raptor said suspiciously. "It doesn't make any sense. Why would you care about destroying his research? If you did all this, it would leave Elysium basically defenseless."

"WE DON'T CARE ABOUT ELYSIUM!" the Guardian leader roared, his patience wearing thin. "Mathison has us bound as slaves with invisible chains. He forces us to do his dirty work. We won't allow him, or his successor, to do that to others any longer. We want nothing more than to be free of him and that cursed city! Let the citizens choose another leader. We'll be long gone."

Raptor and his companions remained silent for a moment as they worked through all the angles of the agreement. Suddenly, Braedon spoke up. "But with Elysium in chaos, the city will be easy targets for Imam Ahmed and his army."

Prometheus turned his attention to the former soldier from Elysium. "Ah yes. Braedon Lewis, the traitor. You and Mr. Lueschen have caused quite a bit of chaos yourselves. You needn't worry about the people in the city. With Elysium on the western side of the Well and Bab al-Jihad on the eastern side, Ahmed would have to take his army through Dehali to get to it. By neutralizing the threat from Elysium, General Ranjit could put most of his resources to defending his eastern flank."

"And what about the disruptor, after you dispose of Mathison?" Raptor asked, interrupting the current conversation. "What guarantee do you expect me to give to Ranjit to convince him that you'll uphold your end of the bargain? In fact, how do we even know this isn't some ploy just to get your hands on Dehali's tech?"

Prometheus turned and nodded toward the black-clad Guardian standing to his right. Virus nodded in return and answered the question. When he spoke, his voice sounded hollow and metallic from the filter in his helmet. "You can instruct the Dehali technicians to place a self-destruct timer into the device. Once we have completed our task, they can fry its entire inner workings. However, they must NOT use explosives. The sensors in the governor's mansion would be able to detect it."

"And I'm sure you wouldn't want to take the chance that they'd decide to blow you up with it," Raptor added wryly.

"Yes. That too."

"Wait a minute," Braedon said as he took a step forward to stand next to Raptor at the front of the group. "If you really plan to take out Mathison and destroy his research in exchange for just using the disruptor, why even offer to help us rescue Gunther and Travis at all?"

With the exception of Kianna and Catrina, the rest of his companions shot him a look of irritation for revealing a favorable flaw in the deal.

However, Prometheus was immediately prepared with an answer, as if he had expected the question. "Because we don't want the imam to get the Vortex technology. This attack will also give us a chance to test his strength and disrupt his plans. With the earthquake straining his resources, now is the perfect chance for a surgical strike that will weaken his power."

Although it seemed that all objections had been answered, Raptor still remained skeptical and unnerved by the details. "So what happens if Ranjit rejects the deal?"

The corner of Prometheus's dark lip curled slightly. "Then we complete our original mission."

Standing at the back of the group, Catrina paled visibly and drew a little closer to Kianna's side as she cast a furtive glance over her shoulder at the other visored and armored Guardian.

"I need to talk to my team before I give our answer," Raptor said.

"You have two minutes."

When the Guardians made no move to indicate they would give Raptor and the others privacy for their discussion, Raptor opened a TC channel to Jade, Charon, and Xavier. Left out of the loop, Braedon, Kianna, and Catrina were forced to watch as the others held their silent conversation. As the minutes passed, the air seemed to grow heavier with the stillness. The Guardians remained unmoving, likely engaged in their own private conversation while the unfocused eyes of Raptor and his team made them appear hypnotized or possessed.

Finally, after the allotted time had expired, Raptor's gaze regained its focus and he faced the Guardian leader. "Fine. You haven't left us much of a choice, so I guess we'll do things your way. I'll get your message to my contact immediately."

Prometheus merely nodded.

"Ranjit's going to need to confer with his staff before replying," Raptor continued. "So, while we wait, it would be nice if we could get something to eat. It's been a busy, and stressful, day."

"Specter, take them to the kitchen. We've cleared out most of the debris. You can eat and rest there."

The Guardian standing at the back of the group motioned for the others to follow him as he moved down the corridor to the right. The group followed him, noting as they did so that the other Cyborg and the Hybrid Guardians fell silently into step behind them.

After making their way through the partially collapsed building, they emerged into a medium-sized room that appeared to have been some sort of kitchen or break room for employees. A few tables and chairs remained, as well as a row of cabinets set over a long counter.

"You will all sleep here," Specter said without inflection. "This is the largest of the intact rooms. We will escort three of you to your vehicle to retrieve your personal items. After that, you will be confined to this room. All of your weapons will be confiscated. Be warned that we are watching you always. If you attempt to leave, we won't hesitate to use lethal force."

Charon seemed about to complain about the accommodations, but changed his mind after he caught sight of Raptor's expression of warning. Ignoring the exchange, Specter continued. "Those who will get your items from the vehicle must come with us now."

It was quickly decided that Charon, Raptor, and Jade would grab the gear. The three followed the Guardians out of the room. As they walked, Charon opened a TC channel to Raptor and began complaining. Lost in his own thoughts, Raptor tuned out his friend, remembering on occasion to offer a vague reply to his rants.

Despite all of Charon's objections and misgivings, even Raptor failed to admit to himself the true reason for his own concern. Deep down, he believed Stephen's prophecy was true. If Ranjit agreed to the terms, it would take him another three and a half days to get the implant disruptor to Bab al-Jihad.

That meant that when it arrived, he would only have four more days to live.

18

WAITING

It didn't take long for General Ranjit to reply to Raptor's proposal, once he was convinced that it was indeed legitimate. Raptor knew that the man would be a fool to pass up on the offer. Dehali had much to gain and little to nothing to lose. As expected, he informed Raptor that his people would install a microphone in the device. If it was disabled, or if the device was being tampered with in any way, the circuits would fry themselves beyond recognition. Once the Guardians used it to eliminate Mathison, they would fry it anyway. Only two hours after their initial contact, the Dehali military commander contacted Raptor to inform him that the implant disruptor was on its way. Unfortunately, due to the recent earthquakes, several of the train routes that ran throughout Tartarus were blocked, meaning it would have to be transported by car. Instead of taking a mere twelve hours by train, it would now arrive in just over three days.

Three days of waiting.

Sure, they spent several hours creating a plan of attack, and the Guardians agreed to let Raptor and Jade venture into the city on occasion to pick up some supplies. But most of the time was spent waiting around inside the lower level of the broken-down building.

The tension in the kitchen area was thick, both from the impending assault on the Golden Dome compound, and from having Braedon in close proximity to Charon. The larger man's already elevated level of animosity toward the soldier was enhanced by Catrina's emotional instability and idiosyncrasies. Had it not been for Jade's empathy for the woman and the Guardians' constant surveillance, Raptor believed that Charon would have spontaneously combusted from all the pent-up frustration. Even with Jade defending Catrina, Raptor feared that a serious dispute would arise at any moment. The last thing they needed right now was for Prometheus to decide they weren't worth the trouble and simply eliminate them.

Fortunately, Raptor had managed to convince the Guardian leader to allow Braedon and Catrina to use the small storage closet next to the kitchen as their own private quarters. That move succeeded in lowering the stress level considerably.

With nothing else to do to pass the time, Raptor resumed his reading of the digital journal Steven had given to him before his death, despite the often disturbing and conflicting thoughts and emotions the written words aroused within him. Based on Jade's use of her downtime, it appeared that she was engrossed in the same task of reading the copy of the journal he had given her.

Charon, however, was another story. Sometimes, just when Raptor was in the middle of wrestling with some profound concept or deep thought, Charon would interrupt and challenge him to a game of three-dimensional Labyrinth chess. Over their many years of friendship, the two had come to develop a love for the game and had spent countless hours mentally sparring. Although many dismissed Charon's intellect due to his size and strength, Raptor knew otherwise. The big man frequently chose to play dumb to fool his opponent into underestimating him. But in reality, he was shrewd and cunning.

Unlike regular chess, this holographic version had three boards that hovered over each other. Designed to represent the tunnels within the dangerous Labyrinth, characters from the upper and lower levels could attack the middle board, and vice versa. Having to process moves from figures in all three levels simultaneously in a three-dimensional environment often taxed Raptor's mental capacities—which is exactly why he loved the game, especially when he needed to take his mind off of his current situation.

Unfortunately, in this case, the game was robbed of some of its enjoyment because it became a nagging reminder that they might soon find themselves in the *real* Labyrinth.

During a particularly unsatisfying match on the first day of waiting, Raptor looked up from the holographic display as the door to the kitchen opened and Braedon and Catrina entered. Charon, lost in contemplating his next move, merely gave the pair a quick glance and a mumbled curse before returning his focus to the game.

The couple moved purposefully toward the food-preparation area after offering a quick greeting to Kianna, who sat near the far wall, and a general hello to the rest. Although just about everyone else in the room seemed to have returned to their previous activities, Raptor let his gaze linger. There appeared to be tension between the two. Frustration and sadness were written on Braedon's rugged features, while Catrina was clearly on edge and looked like a caged animal. Both appeared extremely weary, yet not physically so. It was an emotional weariness that hung on them like a damp garment.

Raptor watched them and sorted through the myriad of thoughts that passed through his mind, which ranged from confusion to irritation to envy. He was just about to return to his competition with Charon when four loud sounds filled the room in quick succession.

The first sound was that of creaking and groaning metal as a mild aftershock shook the damaged building. The second was the sound of Catrina crying out in fright, followed rapidly by a shout of pain from Braedon. The final sound was that of the bowl that had moments before been holding hot soup crashing to the floor.

As soon as Catrina's eyes fell upon Braedon's pain-filled expression, she began to tremble. Wilting onto the floor, she instinctively held her arm over her head, as if to shield herself from the blows she believed would be coming. Weeping uncontrollably, she began to plead. "I'm sorry! I'm so sorry! Please don't...don't hit me! I...I promise I'll be more careful next time!"

All movement in the room ceased as everyone stared in surprise at the woman. Braedon, still wincing from the burning liquid, knelt down next to his wife and reached out to comfort her. "Cat, it's okay. I'm not going to hurt you."

Peeking under her raised arm, Catrina seemed to realize that she wasn't about to be attacked for her mistake. Her eyes darted around the room and her fear was instantly replaced by self-loathing and shame. Leaping to her feet, she ran out room, followed immediately by her husband.

For several seconds, no one spoke as the stunned onlookers slowly began to process what had just occurred. Finally, Charon broke the silence, his voice oozing irritation. "I don't know what's worse: waiting around for this building to fall down on top of us, or having to deal with those two around. That guy's such an idiot! I would've given up on her a long time ago."

The others in the room looked over at the mercenary in shock at his brazenness. Charon returned their steely gazes. "Oh, c'mon. Don't give me those self-righteous looks. I'm sorry, but no woman is worth that much time and effort. Why doesn't he just move on to the next one? She's clearly damaged goods.

I certainly wouldn't put up with that mess. She's gonna drive him crazy. Did you see him? He's already half there."

The two women in the room narrowed their eyes at him menacingly. Jade insulted him with a highly colorful and inappropriate expletive, while Kianna merely shook her head and stated, "You obviously know nothing about real love."

"I know as much as I want to know," Charon replied, unfazed by their responses. "I don't have time or energy to waste on emotional attachments, sweetheart."

"Then I pity you even more. For if you don't love anyone, then you truly have nothing to live for."

"Spare me your religious philosophies," he spat back. "I got plenty to live for: namely pleasure. And from what I see, my lifestyle has led to quite a bit more pleasure than your buddy's lifestyle. Here's something else for you to philosophize about: if your God is so good and loving, then why would he allow this to happen to Braedon? Why does he allow suffering at all? Why would he allow an innocent like Catrina, or any of the countless other women and children who've been abused, to be sold into slavery? He sure doesn't sound like a very compassionate God to me. He's definitely not one I want to give my allegiance to, much less worship."

"All right, Charon," Raptor intervened. "You've made your point."

"No, it's okay," Kianna countered. "He asked a fair question, and it deserves a fair answer. In fact, I've asked the same question myself."

The others seemed surprised by her candid admission. However, before any of them could recover their voices, she continued, her face expressionless as her mind pried open the long-buried memories of her painful past. "Back when I was in high school, my best friend Cheryl met this guy who seemed to be everything she ever wanted. He was handsome, smart, witty, charming, and fun. But despite all that, I felt that something just didn't seem right about him. I tried to warn Cheryl, but she didn't listen.

"One day, she told me that he had invited her to travel with him to Dehali. I tried to convince her not to go, but she wouldn't listen." Kianna paused, her eyes welling up with tears. "After that, she disappeared. We...we found out later that the guy was a trafficker. He became everything she felt she wanted and needed in a man in order to earn her trust."

Kianna paused to wipe away a tear from her cheek. Fighting past the lump in her throat, she continued her story.

"Shortly after graduation, I moved to Dehali to work with those fighting against trafficking, and to see if I could find out what had happened to Cheryl. I met my husband, Devnath, there. He was a computer technician who specialized in hacking into computers, and he taught me everything he knew. With his help, we eventually located and rescued Cheryl from her 'husband' with the help of members of Crimson Liberty. However, she was so traumatized by abuse that, within a week, she took her own life."

Raptor, Jade and Xavier were so stunned by Kianna's revelations that they could do nothing but sit in silence as she began to cry softly. Charon, however, frowned, his expression one of feigned indifference. "But it didn't end there," Kianna continued, her voice breaking. "Cheryl's captors found where we were staying and...attacked us. I managed to escape with our six-year-old daughter, Alayna, but they...they murdered Devnath. After his death, I sent Alayna back to Elysium to live with her grandparents. To this day I don't know what happened to the men who killed Devnath."

For the first time since beginning her tale, Kianna looked around at the others, her red eyes filled with pain and determination. "So you see, Charon, I'm no stranger to pain and suffering, and I've asked God why he allowed all these things many, many times. Why did he allow Cheryl to fall into the hands of those men? Why did he bring me a great husband, only to allow him to be killed? Why does my daughter have to grow up without her father?"

"But didn't you just prove Charon's point?" Raptor replied. "If that's the way God treats his own believers, then why believe in him at all? Doesn't it just make more sense to believe that evil just happens because there's no God running things?"

"At one point, I felt the same way and I almost lost my faith," Kianna said as she wiped the tears away. "But Stephen helped me answer those questions. God didn't create evil. He created the *possibility* of evil by creating humans with free will. He wanted us to *choose* to love him, which, if you think about it, is the very definition of love: it can't be forced. But if we have the ability to choose, then there *must* be the possibility that we'll chose *not* to love him.

"And if we're truly free to choose, then we're also free to choose to do things which are wrong. The men who sold and bought Cheryl and Catrina *chose* to do evil. The men who murdered my husband *chose* to do evil."

"Then why doesn't God *stop* them from doing evil to innocents?" Jade said, her own eyes filled with pain and bitterness. "Why didn't God stop my husband from beating me, even though I cried out for him to do so many, many times? And why does he often allow them to go unpunished for their crimes? Why didn't he punish the men who killed your husband?"

Kianna nodded in sympathy. "I've asked that question as well. As with any complicated issue, the answers are also complicated and multifaceted."

"Translation: my explanation is so convoluted that it doesn't even make sense to me!" Charon interjected.

The dark-skinned woman's face darkened even further. "You started this! Don't judge my explanation until you've heard it." Charon rolled his eyes but didn't respond. Turning her attention back to Jade, she continued. "There *are* answers. With regards to your first point, what would happen if God stepped in every time someone was going to do something wrong?"

Jade frowned. "There'd be no evil or suffering. That would be a whole lot better than the miserable existence that so many have to endure."

"Yes, but there'd also be no free will. Everyone would be living under a dictatorship as prisoners, forced to comply with his laws because they don't have any other choice. That's not love, that's coercion."

Caught up in the conversation, Kianna looked at them intensely, her emotions raw. "Besides, you need to realize that death isn't the end of the story. Even if those men who murdered my husband are never held accountable for their crime in this life, they will in the next."

"Even if we were to buy all that nonsense, that still doesn't explain earthquakes and natural disasters," Charon shot back. "No one chose those."

"Not directly. But the way Christians understand the origin of the universe, we live in a fallen and broken world because of the choices of the first man and woman." Charon rolled his eyes again at this pronouncement. Seeing that he was about to make a comment, Kianna cut him off. "If I stole the Spelunker and scratched it, dented it, and broke the headlights, would that be your fault? After all, you're the owner."

Her question diverted Charon's original comment and redirected his train of thought. "Yeah, and you wouldn't like what I'd do to you if you ever did something like that!"

A little unnerved by his reply, Kianna nevertheless expounded on her point. "Exactly. In the same way, God made this world perfect and entrusted humans with it. We're the ones that messed it up by our poor choices. I wouldn't be surprised to learn someday that many 'natural' disasters are the results of humans messing with things they don't fully understand.

"But an even bigger point may be the unpopular truth that pain and suffering can sometimes bring about good."

"What?" Charon snickered. "That's one of the stupidest things I've ever heard. You Christians have to do so many mental gymnastics in order to make your religion make sense that you don't even know which way is up anymore."

"There you go again," Kianna scolded, her voice filled with fiery indignation. "Are you going to insult me and dismiss my argument outright like a simpleton, or are you going to actually hear me out and judge my position based on logic and reason like an intelligent person?"

Xavier let out a guffaw and leaned back in his chair. "Dang! She just wrecked you! Let's see you get out of that verbal headlock!"

Charon scowled, then cocked his head to the side, accepting the challenge. "Fine. Let's hear your twisted logic."

"Okay. So, answer me this: when you work out and lift weights, are you sore the next day?"

"Yeah. So?"

"So, you feel pain in the short term, but the pain is making you stronger. Or what about if you cut yourself? Pain tells you that something is wrong so you can bind up the wound. What would happen if you couldn't feel pain when you got a serious gash?"

"You'd bleed to death, probably."

"Wouldn't you say that pain is a good thing?"

Charon narrowed his eyes. "Maybe."

"All pain, whether it's physical, emotional, or psychological, tells us that something is wrong so that we can fix it. It's a warning light. And, as with the case of working out, pain often makes us stronger. When we're in the middle of trauma, we can't see how anything good can come of the situation. But when we look back, we can see that our trials often mature us and make us stronger, if we let them. God cares more about our character than our comfort.

"Another positive is that it's often those who have gone through difficulties that are the best suited to help others through similar circumstances," Kianna continued. "Because I lost Cheryl, I learned more about how people process traumas. I've been able to use that information to help Braedon understand what Catrina's going through. Because Cheryl was abducted, I dedicated myself to rescuing other women. And I can say that, because of my work and the work of many others, we've been able to rescue over one hundred women—saving them from a life of misery. If it hadn't been for my pain, I may never have even become aware of their plight and they might still be stuck in that suffering."

Kianna paused, as if deciding how far to push the subject. Finally making her decision, she plunged ahead. "Ultimately, the most horrible suffering produced the greatest good. By dying on the cross for our sins, Jesus suffered so that we can all have eternal life. We Christians don't serve some high-and-mighty God who sits on his throne and watches the toils and travails of his creations with detached indifference. But our God loved us so much he paid the price for our disobedience."

"Save your preaching for those who care," Charon spat. "I get your general point, but it still seems to me like a bunch of philosophical mumbo-jumbo. Maybe the reason there's suffering in this wretched world is that there's no God in the first place. It's just survival-of-the-fittest evolution."

Kianna's expression saddened. "Do you realize, Charon, that if you're right, then there's no such thing as 'good' either? If we're all just cosmic accidents, then love, compassion, kindness, et cetera, are just wasted efforts. In fact, we wouldn't even have free will, because our actions would just be the results of chemical interactions within our brains. Does it make sense to punish hydrogen and oxygen for bonding together to form water? That's just what they do. They're chemicals. They don't have a choice. So, if we're just the result of random chemicals, then a person's actions are just the result of random chemicals mixing in the brain. There is no right or wrong, good or evil."

"Whoa, that's pretty deep," Xavier frowned. "My head hurts just trying to figure that one out."

"You can believe in your benevolent, fairy-tale deity if it makes you feel better when you stub your toe, but I'm a realist," Charon said. "If belief in evolution means no right or wrong, then I'll just have to swallow that bitter pill, not try to make up some mixed-up belief system in order to explain it away. Anyway, I've had enough of this conversation. So, if you don't mind, I'd like to get back to my game." He turned his chair noisily to face the holographic chess game, sending the obvious message to Kianna that he was finished talking. A second later, he moved one of his pawns and signaled toward Raptor. "Your turn."

Although Kianna and the others let the conversation drop, Raptor couldn't get his mind to return fully to the game. The whole incident with Braedon and Catrina, as well as Kianna's revelations and explanations, continued to plague him. He agreed with Charon in principle, but he had also never encountered a man who was as unselfish, forgiving, and patient as Braedon. *I can find ways to deny the man's beliefs, but can I deny his actions?* Raptor wondered. Despite his best efforts to lose himself in the labyrinthine movements of the chess game, his mind somehow kept finding its way back to thoughts of how things might have turned out differently if only the people in his life had held the beliefs of Braedon and Kianna, and, more importantly, acted upon those beliefs.

19

THE HOUND OF HEAVEN

Raptor, I need to talk to you.

The TeleConnect message was from Braedon. With his imagination unwillingly jumping to half a dozen conclusions as to the topic of the forthcoming conversation, Raptor sighed in newfound frustration. *What does he want now?* he thought as he turned off the holographic map of the Labyrinth. He sent a quick mental command to his implant, which dialed up a connection. A moment later, Braedon responded.

Thanks for getting back to me.

Sure. What do you want? he replied, his frustration bleeding into the digitized version of his voice.

I want to talk to you about Catrina.

There it was. Raptor figured that even if she wasn't the main topic of conversation, somehow it would end up moving in this direction. He let out a mumbled curse before replying. *Look, you know where I stand. I'm not going to—*

Kianna and I have convinced Cat to take something to help her sleep through the whole mission, if she feels she can't take the stress.

Raptor didn't respond as he took in this new development. Hearing nothing but silence, Braedon decided to continue. *I believe the best solution would be to have Kianna and Cat stay in the Spelunker on the outskirts of the city. Kianna can still hack into the security systems from there, and Cat can keep her company. Besides, we may want to have someone ready to pick us up in the Spelunker and to keep the Vortex weapon safe, especially if things turn ugly.*

Xavier was going to take that job.

Fine. But I still think having Cat and Kianna with him is the best option.

And what about you?

I want in on the operation.

Although part of him didn't want the Christian man along, Raptor's logic won out. In fact, he was inwardly relieved. He hated to admit it, even to himself, but he needed the man's intelligence and fighting skills if they were going to pull this off.

Okay. But you follow my orders. Understood? And I need to know that your mind will be focused. I can't have anyone getting shot because you were distracted trying to check up on your wife.

Yeah, I get it. I won't let anything get in my way.

Good.

In fact, I have my own concerns about you. After all, your father's the leader of this army. These are your people. You may have grown up with some of them. How do I know that you won't let your own personal feelings interfere? What if we run into your father himself? What then?

Raptor snickered unconvincingly. *Let me assure you, that's the last thing you need to worry about. What bonds I once had with my father, or anyone else in this city for that matter, have long been broken.*

In many ways, I'm sorry to hear that. I don't know what happened to you, but it usually takes some major tragedy or argument to cause a person to walk away from everyone and everything they knew.

Braedon's reply surprised Raptor and stirred up unwelcome memories. *Well, in this case it works to your benefit. We'll work you into the plan.*

Thanks. Listen, I have one more thing I'd like to ask.

What now? Raptor found himself growing increasingly impatient.

If…if anything happens to me, would you please help Cat and Kianna get to someplace safe?

Somewhat taken aback by the request, Raptor hesitated before responding. *Sure. If there's anywhere "safe" to get to. Now, if you don't mind, I'm going to get some sleep. The package from Dehali arrives tomorrow, so it'll likely be a very busy day.*

Without even waiting for the other to respond, Raptor shut down the connection. Although he truly wanted to get some rest, he knew it would likely be hours before he fell asleep. Leaning against the wall of the food-prep room, he frowned. *What is it about that guy that bugs me so much?* he wondered. *I get irritated just talking to him.*

Maybe it's because you admire him.

The thought caught him off guard. Brushing it aside lest he consider the possibility that it might be true, he sought something to distract him. With everyone else asleep on their makeshift beds, Raptor found his options quite limited. He considered going back to studying the map of the Labyrinth, but somehow he knew it would only stir up images of his nightmare. Instead, he flipped on Steven's journal, hoping to find solace in his former mentor's logic and reasoning.

My sons,

At this point, I've tried to show you several ways in which I believe that Christianity best explains reality and is unique among the religions of the world. But one area that I've failed to touch on is the motive of the founder and the origin of the religion. Just like in a court case, one needs to examine whether the accused had a reason for committing the crime and study the details of how it occurred. In the same way, we can examine how each religion came about to search for any ulterior motives from the founder, and study the circumstances around which it began. Did he have anything to gain? Power? Wealth? Status? What was going on in the culture when the religion came into being? All of these might call into question the truth of the person's claims.

Take Muhammad and Islam for example. In the seventh century, around 610 BC, Muhammad supposedly received a visit from the angel Gabriel. These visitations formed the basis of the Qur'an. The basic message from Gabriel was that the Bible had originally contained the truth from Allah, but had become corrupted. Therefore, Gabriel had been sent to give the truth to him. According to Muhammad, many of the Old Testament patriarchs, such as Adam, Noah, and Abraham, were considered to originally be Muslims. However, he taught that one of the greatest errors in the Hebrew Torah (the first five books of the Old Testament) is that it wasn't Abraham's son Isaac that was the chosen one of God but rather his son Ishmael. It is this belief that forms one of the greatest rifts between the Jewish people and the Muslims.

I hope I didn't lose you with too many details. The main point is that there are several beliefs of Islam that cause one to question Muhammad's motives. For one, Muslims believe that the Arabic form of the Qur'an is pure and has been kept from corruption by Allah for well over one thousand years. But that begs the question: if Allah could keep the Qur'an from corruption, and if the Bible was originally uncorrupted, then why didn't he keep the Bible from corruption in the first place, which would negate the need for the Qur'an?

Another belief that raises red flags is that of abrogation. The Qur'an teaches that later pronouncements of Muhammad nullify or void his earlier pronouncements. But again, this begs a question: if God is all-knowing, why would he change his mind? On the other hand, if you compare the teachings of Muhammad to the events in his life, you see an interesting correlation. In the early part of his teaching, when he had very few followers, his messages were more peaceful and less controversial. However, as he gained more and more power, his rules became stricter, his doctrine more hostile toward unbelievers.

It is also interesting to note that Islam isn't the only religion to have been founded by a man who supposedly received a revelation from an angel stating that the Bible had been corrupted. In the year 1823, according to the Earth calendar, in the state of New York in the United States of America, a man named Joseph Smith claimed that he received a visitation from an angel named Moroni. This angel told young Joseph, who was only seventeen years old at the time, that the New Testament from the Bible had been corrupted. The angel then told him where to find a set of golden plates that contained the truth about Jesus and God. Moroni then visited Joseph every year for four years to instruct him on how to read the plates and translate them into English. This became the Book of Mormon and Joseph Smith founded the Church of Jesus Christ of the Latter-day Saints—also known as the Mormons.

The Mormons believe that God was once human, and when we die, we may become like God if we follow the teachings of the church. Although this is in stark contrast to the teachings of Islam, it is interesting to note that in the New Testament book of Galatians, Paul the apostle writes this in the first chapter:

> I am astonished that you are so quickly deserting the one who called you to live in the grace of Christ and are turning to a different gospel—which is really no gospel at all. Evidently some people are throwing you into confusion and are trying to pervert the gospel of Christ. But even if we or an angel from heaven should preach a gospel other than the one we preached to you, let them be under God's curse! As we have already said, so now I say again: If anybody is preaching to you a gospel other than what you accepted, let them be under God's curse!

Raptor paused his reading, overwhelmed with shock. He'd heard the story of Muhammad's angelic visitation many times, but he never knew that the Mormon religion had such a similar story. *How is it that two religions could have nearly identical foundations AND both claim that the Bible was corrupted? And could it simply be coincidence that this very possibility was warned against hundreds of years prior?* The questions pounded their way past Raptor's mental defenses, destroying his preconceived notions. Despite his best efforts to the contrary, he was compelled to return to the journal entry.

> While Muhammad and Joseph Smith gained power, prestige, and multiple wives for their efforts, what did Jesus and his disciples gain? Jesus was beaten, battered, and crucified. His disciples were also beaten, flogged, and persecuted. And, with the exception of the apostle John, they were all martyred for their faith.

Furthermore, consider this comparison. Nearly every other religion—Buddhism, Islam, Mormonism, Jehovah's Witnesses, etc.—started with a private revelation to one person that was then spread publicly. Christianity, in stark contrast, started out as public events (death and resurrection of Jesus) that spread publicly.

You see, my sons, unlike every other religion, Christianity isn't just a set of teachings: it is based on historic events. In fact, you could replace the founder of every other religion and the religion remains intact. Why? Because the other religions are sets of rules, regulations, and laws. But what happens if you take away Jesus from Christianity? You have nothing! If Jesus didn't truly pay for our sins by dying on the cross, then we are still sinful. And if he didn't rise again, then how can we truly believe he was telling the truth that he was God?

Think about it. Even though the Qur'an teaches that Muhammad was a greater prophet than Jesus, it attributes miracles to Jesus, but not to Muhammad. We also have the graves of Buddha, Muhammad, Joseph Smith, Charles Russell, etc. But the grave of Jesus is empty!

The Christian Bible contains the entire Jewish scripture (called the Old Testament), which are all based in history that has been proven time and time again by archaeology. But even more, the New Testament contains the writings of those who were eyewitnesses of the events of Jesus's birth and resurrection.

Again, using the court analogy, whom would you rather believe: a single man with no witnesses or supporting evidence, or multiple men who were eyewitnesses of public events that can be corroborated with logic and archaeology?

I hope by now you have come to realize that my beliefs are not based solely on faith but also on reason. In fact, my beliefs are the next logical step in a long line of reasoning. God does not expect us to have blind faith. He has given us enough in his creation to make belief in him reasonable, but has left out enough so that it is impossible to live with reason alone.

My sons, the choice is yours. But I plead with you to keep in mind that making no decision for Christ is making a decision. You can't remain neutral between the prosecuting attorney and the judge!

I love you, and pray with all my being that my words might remove whatever stumbling blocks are keeping you from accepting the free gift of eternal life that is offered by Jesus's sacrifice.

Your loving father

Shutting off the holographic reader, Raptor lay back on his pillow. The ever-elusive sleep didn't overtake him for nearly another hour. When it did, he dreamt once more. However, instead of the recurring nightmare of being chased through dark tunnels by a vicious dragon, this time, he was being chased by the hound of heaven.

20

CATCHING A RIDE

Here it comes, right on schedule. It sure is a good thing you knew about this truck.

Raptor smiled at Xavier's comment. *Yeah, well that's what happens when you grow up in this city. I remember these delivery trucks bringing supplies to the compound once a week when I was in classes there.*

Wow. I guess it's a good thing they haven't changed their delivery schedule in all these years. Uh…not that I'm calling you old or anything.

I'm not old, I'm experienced. And, for your information, they did *change their schedule,* Raptor replied. *I had Kianna do a little snooping around and she found the new schedule and itinerary.*

Ah, I see.

The lumbering truck rolled down the wide, abandoned alley on its ten wheels and came to a stop right where Raptor and Charon were hiding.

Okay, everyone. Stay sharp.

From their vantage point, they could see clearly through the front window of the vehicle. As expected, the two occupants looked disoriented and wore expressions of complete surprise and bewilderment.

Those expressions only deepened as a man dressed in a full black bodysuit and helmet materialized next to the driver's door and yanked it open. At the same time, Charon and Raptor threw off their digital invisibility cloaks and followed suit on the opposite side of the vehicle. Within a matter of seconds, the two men were lying unconscious in the alleyway.

Xavier and Braedon came out of concealment a moment later and helped move the bodies off to the side. With quiet efficiency, Raptor and the others removed any useful items, bound the men, and concealed them behind several large crates.

"That should do it," Xavier commented as he rubbed his hands together in satisfaction. "With the dose I gave them, they should sleep until well after we're gone from the city."

"And Kianna reports that there's no sign of any alerts sent out in the military TC feeds. It seems that the Implant Disruptor did its job," Braedon announced.

Xavier put his hand to his head. "That's for sure. I know we turned it on a couple of times to test it and to help us adjust to its effects, but it still turns my brain to Jell-O."

"Let's get moving before some local idiot stumbles upon us," Raptor said and glanced down the alley to search for any signs that their activities had been noticed. Seeing nothing amiss, he turned to face the Cyborg. "Thanks for your help, Specter. Let Prometheus know that we're heading toward the bridge."

"Already done," came the cold reply. A second later, the technologically altered human activated his suit's own version of the invisibility cloak and disappeared. The thousands of microscopic cameras embedded into the back of his armored uniform projected their images onto the front until only a vague hazy shape of a man was left. Moments later, the haze disappeared down the alley and was lost from sight.

"Friendly chap, isn't he?" Braedon stated sarcastically.

"Yeah. But there's no denying the efficiency of those Guardians," Charon commented. "I feel much better knowing that, at least for now, they're on our side."

"No kidding, right?" Xavier replied. "I don't know what kind of gadget Virus gave Specter, but it sure did the trick. Did you see the look on those workers' faces when their computer driver suddenly changed course and led them into our trap? And with those camouflage suits and their sticky, Spiderman gripping ability, it's no wonder the Guardians are so hard to catch."

"In this case, those are the very attributes that are going to make this job a lot easier," Raptor said. "Now load up and let's get this over with."

Xavier and Raptor moved over to the back of the truck and opened the doors while Braedon and Charon grabbed the large satchels containing their weapons and gear, as well as the two cloaks. Climbing into the back of the truck, Braedon and Charon slipped between the stacks of supplies and made their way to the front. Once they were crouched down and hidden, with cloaks wrapped around them to further conceal them from view, Raptor and Xavier closed the back doors. With everything in place, the two climbed into the front of the truck and reengaged the computer driver.

Once they were safely on their way, Xavier turned causally toward Raptor. "By the way, Braedon mentioned to me some nonsense about you having me babysit Kianna and 'sleeping beauty' in the Spelunker. What was that all about?"

Raptor laughed. "I was just messin' with him. I couldn't afford to have you stay behind."

Although somewhat reassured, Xavier wasn't completely convinced. "That's good to know. I mean, I didn't *think* you'd ever consider leaving me behind. But then again, I thought maybe it was because you were concerned about leaving our 'prized possession' in the care of a religious zealot. Aren't you even a little concerned that Kianna will take the Vortex weapon?"

"Not likely. Braedon's got them both convinced that Gunther and Travis are the only ones who can use it to reverse the portals, and that if they can't, we're all gonna die anyway."

"And you don't buy into that?"

Raptor paused. "Maybe. I know that's what I told Prometheus. But his response about how the Elysium scientists think it's just a passing wave of rock movement has me thinking. Then again, I don't trust anything that comes out of Elysium, so I'm not sure what to believe."

Xavier let the conversation drop as the vehicle moved closer to the southern bridge. Although the earthquake that shook the city several days ago had filled parts of the bridge with debris, the crews had since cleared most of it away.

"Prometheus was right. They still have two soldiers in mech suits standing guard in addition to the two armed inspectors," Xavier said, a nervous edge to his voice.

"Relax. These supply trucks are routine. The inspectors are probably bored out of their skulls. The most they'll do is pop open the back, glance inside, and wave us through."

"Yeah, as long as Kianna and Virus were able to successfully plant our pictures, fingerprints, dental records, shoe size, and whatever other forms of identification these paranoid military types require," Xavier stated. "I mean, these disguises and uniforms you scrounged up make us *look* the part, but if our IDs don't show up…what if…what if Prometheus deliberately had Virus set us up so the guards would capture us and—"

"Quit your whining!" Raptor interrupted. "I don't know what's worse, your worrying or Charon's grumbling! Next time, I think I *will* leave you with the women!"

"Ha, ha. I'm just trying to think of all the possibilities."

"Believe me, I've thought this through. Trust me."

Xavier threw him a sideways look full of skepticism and sarcasm. "That's what you said just before that fiasco with the Sorian Industries night patrol. How much did that disaster cost us, again?"

Raptor grimaced. "I don't remember."

His companion smiled widely. "Right. You know, repressing memories can lead to insanity."

"I'll be sure to remember that," Raptor said with a grin before turning serious. "Okay, master thespian, get into character. It's show time."

The computer program driving the vehicle brought the truck to a halt several feet in front of the heavy metal gate that barred entrance to the bridge. As predicted, the two guards in the mech suits that framed the gate appeared to be just slightly less than completely bored with the approach of the delivery truck. The expressions on the faces of the two inspectors that approached the driver's side door showed a bit more interest, but it was clear they had gone through these procedures numerous times.

Without a word, the first inspector raised a handheld scanner. Raptor and Xavier kept their heads motionless as the device analyzed their retinas and facial features. A moment later, the man lowered the scanner and nodded affirmatively. "Open the back."

With a mental command from his implant, he activated the switch that opened the back of the truck. He glanced in the side mirrors to see the rear doors of the truck come into view. Seconds later, both inspectors disappeared behind the vehicle.

I hate the waiting, Xavier said through his implant. *I'd rather get caught and have to fight than wait. The suspense is brutal.*

Not bothering to reply, Raptor simply continued his act of matching the bored expressions on the faces of the other men. In order to take his mind off his own anxiety, he casually studied the guards and their mechs.

Each armored suit stood nearly ten feet in height and contained a host of weaponry. Rockets, missiles, lasers, and machine guns were attached to the arms and shoulders. The bodies of the men inside the suits were completely covered. Only their faces were visible through the thick rectangular sheet of darkened glass about two feet wide. And although it wasn't visible to him from his current angle, Raptor knew that each suit came with hoverjets on both legs and on the back, which made it possible to move smoothly and rapidly over various types of terrain.

His perusal of the guards was interrupted a moment later when the two inspectors appeared once more. Immediately, Raptor felt his pulse quicken. *Something's wrong,* he told Xavier through the implant. With his heart pounding, he watched as the first inspector waved to one of the guards. The man quickly activated his suit and within moments was standing near the back of the truck.

Do we go to plan B? Xavier asked.

No, not yet. Charon and Braedon would have notified us if they'd been discovered. Maybe it'll turn out to be something as simple as a loose crate.

Sure, Xavier replied sarcastically as his right hand slid beneath his jacket and withdrew one of the EMP grenades. Despite his assurances, Raptor felt his own hand reaching for his concealed laser pistol. As he did so, he opened a TC channel to Charon and Braedon. *What's going on?*

We don't know, Charon replied. *We can't see from where we're hidden. Wait a second...the inspector's coming this way!*

Raptor's grip on his weapon grew tighter as he fought to retain his composure. Although it only took seconds for Charon to reply, it seemed like hours to the men in the cab. *He's...he's heading back to the door. I can't tell if he saw us and is retreating for backup. If we want the element of surprise, we should attack now!*

The pressure of the moment weighed heavily upon Raptor, causing his mind to momentarily freeze up.

Raptor, do we attack? Make a decision!

No! Stay hidden. We may lose the surprise, but we have to make sure... His thought trailed off as he caught sight of the guard's mech suit appear around the corner. Raptor held his breath as the man approached...and passed by the cab. A moment later, the inspectors followed. Splitting up, the first one came back up to Raptor's window.

"Sorry about the delay," the man said. "One of your crates came loose. I had the guard push it back into place and secure it again."

Raptor tried not to let any of his suddenly released anxiety show in his reaction. Instead, he feigned minor impatience. "I'm glad it wasn't anything more serious. We're already behind schedule as it is."

The man nodded and stepped back. The heavy gate in front of the truck began to open slowly, probably from a silent command through one of the inspector's implants. Taking that as his cue, Raptor closed the back doors of the truck and nodded to the men as they headed back to their posts in the guardhouse. Seconds later, the vehicle moved forward onto the bridge.

As the gate and its sentinels faded into the distance, Xavier released his long-held laugh. "I can't believe it actually *was* a loose crate! That never happens!"

Raptor released his own laugh. "Sometimes I amaze even myself. And you were worried about the scanners. I told you they aren't that hard to fool if you know how they work."

Xavier cast him a look of mild respect. "That's why you're the boss, boss."

Raptor quickly filled Charon and Braedon in on what had transpired. As he finished doing so, the truck neared the end of the bridge and approached the compound. Directly ahead lay the small storage building bathed in the light from the Golden Dome perched upon the top of the tower in the center of the island. The other five buildings were built in a rectangular shape along the east and west sides, with the Great Golden Mosque forming the northern edge.

Two of the mechs were stationed on each side of this end of the bridge, exactly like their counterparts on the city proper. Raptor noticed with assurance that the intel provided by the Guardians regarding the position of the other mech guards was precise. All four bridges had a pair of the armored suits on each side, with another pair at each of the four corners of the rectangular compound, making for a total of sixteen. In an emergency, the two at the mainland ends of each bridge could reach the island quickly, bringing the total to twenty-four.

In addition, Raptor counted eight regular guards standing nearby, some on patrol and others working near vehicles. *And who knows how many more just inside the buildings.* Pushing the unpleasant thought from his mind, he focused on his observations.

Once the truck reached the island, the computerized driver piloted the vehicle along a curved service road near where the other pair of guards in mech suits were stationed. It continued along the side of the storage building and came to a stop near the building's loading dock. A few minutes later, it had the back of the truck snuggled up to the platform and ready to be unloaded.

Popping open the back doors once again, Raptor climbed out and headed toward the man in charge of receiving. Per the plan, Xavier remained inside the truck and pretended to be working on his palm-sized holographic computer.

As he conversed with the overseer, Raptor's gaze bounced back and forth between the workers as they began unloading the truck, the four mechs, and the other stray guards. After several minutes, he began to relax as it appeared that all of them had their attention focused on other duties.

During a lull in the unloading process, when none of the men were near the back of the truck, Raptor sent the signal to his concealed companions. A moment later, two shimmering forms exited the truck and disappeared around the sides of the nearby garbage disposal units.

Raptor grinned slightly as he settled in to wait. *So far, so good,* he thought. *This might turn out to be easier than I thought.*

Two hours later, with the globe above dimming into its late evening glow, the crew had nearly finished unloading. While he waited, Raptor opened a TC channel to Jade to check on her progress. However, before he could finish his conversation, the sudden voice of Kianna came through his implant via her implant translator. The urgency in her voice sent his pulse racing.

Raptor! Braedon! Get out of there!

What is it? What's going on? he replied immediately.

Even as his thought was transmitted through the channel, he noticed the four guards standing nearby suddenly activate their robotic suits and begin heading directly toward him.

I don't know how, but their facial-recognition software broke through the layers of code that Virus and I put into place! Raptor, they know you're there!

21

INFILTRATION

Jade couldn't resist the temptation any longer. Opening her eyes, she looked over her shoulder and immediately regretted the choice.

I can't believe I let Raptor talk me into this. I'm gonna die for sure. Mingyu, this is by far the craziest thing you've ever done. At least I know now what it feels like for Zei. I wish she couldn't come along. I could really use her companionship right now. It's too bad she has to wait in the Spelunker.

Shutting out the image of the city far below her, Jade focused instead on hanging onto the back of the Guardian and praying that the straps keeping her in place held. *If not, then at least I'll die quickly.* Death. It had always been a possibility given her current line of work. However, recent events had caused her to give it more thought than usual, and, like Raptor, she didn't particularly care for any of her options.

Pushing aside her unwelcome thoughts, she opened a TC channel to her companion. **Virus, how much farther until we reach the center of the cavern?**

The servos and actuators implanted in the man's muscles kept his arms and legs moving quickly and effortlessly as he continued to climb across the ceiling of the enormous cavern that housed the city of Bab al-Jihad. The arms, hands, feet, and knees of the Guardian's suit were modeled after the suction pads on the feet of geckos. This allowed him to cling to nearly any surface. A simple rolling action was all that was required to release the suction. With practice, the Guardians had learned how to climb just about anything with skill and speed, giving them a definite advantage over their enemies, especially in an underground world.

An advantage that Raptor had decided to exploit.

At our current travel rate, we will arrive at our destination in precisely one minute and twenty-three seconds.

Jade rolled her eyes. *Those crazy Elysium scientists have messed around so much with the brains of these poor guys that I wonder if any humanity is left.* Switching channels, she contacted Raptor. *We're almost there. How are things on your end?*

A few seconds later, his voice echoed in her head. *The workers are almost finished unloading the truck. According to Kianna, there's no sign from the military channels that you and Virus have been spotted. Your invisibility cloak seems to be working. Then again, no one ever looks up, especially not in a huge cavern.*

That's because nobody's stupid enough to try a stunt like this. Oh, wait, nobody except ME! Next time, you can come along for the ride.

Well, with any luck, there won't BE a next...

Raptor let his thought go unfinished as both of their implants alerted them to an incoming urgent message from Kianna. Jade felt her pulse quicken. If it was urgent it probably wasn't going to be good news. With a mental command, Raptor added her to the conversation.

I don't know how, but their facial-recognition software broke through the layers of code that Virus and I put into place! Raptor, they know you're there!

Raptor swore. *Thanks for the heads-up. Jade, we need you in position NOW!*

We're getting ready to drop in a few seconds.

Good. Move quick. We need speed now, not stealth. I'll let the others know that our timetable just got moved up. Good luck.

The moment the connection was broken off, Jade opened a new one to Virus and explained the situation to him. In his typical cold fashion, he didn't respond but merely nodded in understanding. Less than a minute later, he halted his climb.

We have arrived.

With quick, precise movements, the Guardian took out a sturdy climbing anchor and shoved it into the rock ceiling. Seconds later, he attached their harnesses to it.

You are ready to descend.

Although Jade had been through many harrowing situations and didn't really have a fear of heights, she still found herself fighting against the voice screaming in her head telling her not to let go. However, as she had done many times before, she buried her emotions and set her will on her task. With her harness now attached to the cable being fed through the anchor, nothing held her to Virus except her arms and legs. Taking a deep breath, she let go.

The initial plunge terrified her more than she would later admit. As she fell, the horrifying thought resurfaced that perhaps Virus intended her to plummet to her death. Unable to stop herself, she looked down to see the top of the Golden Dome drawing quickly nearer to her right. With her current trajectory, she would pass within three feet of the side of it to land on the topmost balcony of the tower just beneath the glowing sphere. Despite her self-adjusting, light-filtering goggles, Jade was forced to turn her head away from the dome's brilliance.

Then, just as her adrenaline began to morph into panic, she felt her progress begin to slow. By the time she was passing next to the dome, she had slowed down considerably. With precision that could only be attributed to the computerized portion of his brain, Virus brought her to a halt within inches of the floor of the balcony.

Hitting the release on her harness, she dropped into a crouch. Although Raptor would have preferred to infiltrate the compound at night when the dome would be at its dimmest setting, the delivery truck's schedule left them little choice. They pushed the arrival time as far back as they could without raising suspicion. However, the evening setting for the dome still produced enough light that her fuzzy silhouette would likely have been noticed, even with the invisibility cloak wrapped tightly around her. Raptor had hoped that most would dismiss the brief shadow as the falling of a small rock, as is common from time to time. But with the alarm having already been raised, she knew that any halfway-decent military would send someone to investigate.

With that conclusion fresh in her mind, Jade made the decision not to wait even the few seconds it would take for Virus to join her. Instead, she headed toward the door that led into the tower itself and flung it open.

The nearly circular room was roughly thirty feet in diameter and housed several control panels that, according to Raptor, controlled the Golden Dome as well as the sound system used to announce the call to prayer, or the *adhan*, five times each day all over the city. Fortunately, Raptor had planned the attack in between the *Salat al-'asr*, which occurs in the late part of the afternoon, and the *Salat al-Maghrib* just after the dome's "sunset," which meant the room was completely empty.

Rushing over to the control panel on the left, she searched for the switches that Raptor had indicated in their planning sessions. Finding what she was looking for, she opened a TC channel to Raptor. *I'm in position and awaiting your signal!*

No sooner had Raptor finished relaying Kianna's warning to Prometheus than he heard the sound of four of the mech suits approaching. Still playing his role, he casually glanced toward the approaching AAC guards with minimal interest. One of them stopped his mech several feet from where Raptor was leaning against the side of the truck, the weapons on the machine pointed directly at him. One of the other mech pilots moved around the vehicle to aim his own weapons at Xavier, who sat inside the cab, while the remaining two armored guards took up alert positions behind their comrades.

"Rahib Ahmed, by order of the imam, you will remain where you are and allow yourself to be searched," the guard standing nearest him commanded. A moment later, the front of the man's suit opened, allowing him to step out of it. As the man drew nearer, Raptor could see that, in addition to his laser pistol, the man also held a small, Implant Inhibitor, similar to the one Raptor himself had put on Braedon back in Elysium.

With the man's focus on Raptor, he never saw the two EMP grenades roll out from where Charon and Braedon had taken cover behind the stack of crates. A second later, the grenades exploded and released their energy in a flash of orangish light. Strands of crackling electricity lit up the four mech suits, overloading their circuits and shutting them down.

Although the energy wave sent a sharp tingle through his body, the grenades were harmless to humans. Being prepared for the attack, Raptor reacted a split second before the guard could recover from the unexpected attack. With a swift kick, he knocked the weapon out of the man's hand, then followed up with a solid punch to his face, knocking him unconscious.

Grabbing the fallen weapon, Raptor looked up to see the hazy form of Charon, still covered in the invisibility cloak, charging toward the side of the other mech. Just as he arrived, the guard hit the manual release on the suit, causing the front to open. With weapon in hand, he leapt out of it and fired off a shot at the charging attacker. Charon easily dodged the unsteady blast, closed the remaining distance between them, and tackled the man.

Seeing that Charon had the situation under control, Raptor ran around the front of the truck and quickly assessed the situation. As with the guard that approached him, the mech nearest the side of the truck was open, its pilot lying unconscious on the ground, along with two other foot soldiers Xavier had clearly taken out. The second guard, however, had successfully extracted himself from his suit before Braedon could reach him, forcing him to take cover behind the edge of a nearby vehicle. Xavier, on the other hand, was sitting behind the disabled mech of the other guard and holding his left shoulder painfully.

With the last man's attention focused on Braedon, Raptor used the front of the truck to steady his arm, aim, and drop the AAC jihadist with a single shot. Before the man's unconscious body hit the ground, Raptor was crouching by Xavier's side.

"How bad is it?"

"Well, I'm not gonna die," Xavier quipped through clenched teeth, "but it stings worse than a bite from a Razor Fish."

"Trust me, I know how bad those can be," Raptor replied empathetically as his eyes continued to scan the area for signs of other attackers. "But we don't have time for this. Quit bellyaching and let's get going. There are at least six more soldiers nearby, not to mention the other two mechs by the eastern bridge."

Xavier shot him a wry look, which was made all the more comical when combined with his Arab disguise. Grabbing his uninjured right arm, Raptor helped his friend to his feet. A second later, Braedon came running around the corner of the truck to join them, the hood of his cloak thrown back.

"Where's Charon?" Raptor asked, his brow furrowing.

"He's putting the mech suits out of commission permanently."

Just as Braedon finished his explanation, Charon appeared around the back of the truck. After casting a cursory wave in their direction, he proceeded directly to the nearest mech. He ducked his head inside the torso of the machine for a handful of seconds, then reemerged and headed toward his companions.

"I made a few personal 'adjustments' to their toys," Charon commented with a grin. "They won't be able to use them without some serious repair."

"Nice. We've got to get inside before more of them arrive," Raptor replied. "Hold on a second, Jade's checking in." Immediately, his eyes lost their focus as he opened the TC channel. *What's your status?*

I'm in position and awaiting your signal!

Great. Hit it as soon as—

However, before Raptor could finish his sentence, a huge explosion erupted from the other side of the Golden Dome compound, sending dark plumes of smoke floating toward the ceiling of the cavern.

You were saying?

Raptor let a sly grin cross his features at Jade's question. *It looks like our 'friends' have joined the party. No need to wait. Give us ten seconds, then hit it. And don't forget to turn on your commlink.*

Got it, boss. See you at the checkpoint.

"Goggles on, boys," Raptor said to the others as he closed down the connection. "It's about to get a little hard to see."

"Uh, boss—a little help?" Xavier said, nodding toward his wound.

Moving rapidly, Raptor reached into Xavier's pocket, withdrew a set of goggles, and placed them on the man's head before putting on his own.

A moment later, his words were proven prophetic as the brilliant light from the Golden Dome completely ceased, plunging the entire cavern into darkness. At nearly the same instant, the four men felt the uncomfortably familiar sense of disorientation as their implant feeds went dead.

"Ha!" Xavier exclaimed in triumph. "That oughta give these blokes something to worry about!"

"Yeah, let's make sure we make the most of the distraction," Raptor stated. However, just as he was about to sprint away from the area, Charon's voice halted him.

"Raptor, change of plans. I'll meet up with you later."

"What?" Raptor asked with a frown as he turned back around. Noticing the look on his best friend's face, he knew instantly that the big man had something up his sleeve. "Braedon, you and Xavier get moving. I'll be right behind you." Used to following orders, Braedon helped the con man to his feet. Even as the two men hurried off, Charon began explaining his idea.

"I like it," Raptor commented when the other had finished. "Keep your comm on, your head down, and be ready to assist. Good luck."

"You too," Charon replied, a broad smile splitting his rugged features. "Just like old times, huh?"

"Yeah, right." With one last glance at the man who had been his best friend for the past nineteen years, Raptor turned and ran to catch up to the others, who were already making their way in the dark away from the storage building and toward the other structure on the east side of the island.

As he ran, he noticed that lights were gradually beginning to flare to life both inside and outside the buildings all across the city proper. However, the confused occupants of the compound, used to activating the lights with a command from their implants, took nearly a minute to finally locate and activate the manual switches. That minute was all Raptor needed to catch up with the others and reach the back door of the next building.

To the north and west, flashes of light lit up the darkness, accompanied by small explosions and sounds of laser fire. "So far so good," Xavier whispered as they arrived at the door. "Let's just hope this Codebreaker we borrowed from your old buddy Bastian works on industrial-grade locks."

Beside him, Raptor worked frantically to place the small handheld device on the lock of the door. Within the building, more and more bulbs were being lit, their brilliance spilling out the windows to chase away the darkness.

"C'mon, c'mon!" Xavier said nervously as some of the outside security lights flashed on. "I thought Virus had this covered!"

"That was the plan," Raptor hissed through clenched teeth.

"I guess that's what we get for trusting a Guardian!"

"Got it!" Raptor whispered in relief as the light on the Codebreaker turned green and the door lock clicked open. With skill derived from many years of practice, he disconnected the device in a matter of seconds. "Go!"

Without hesitation, Braedon pushed the door open and jumped inside, his laser pistol leading the way, with Xavier right behind him. Raptor leaped inside and slammed the door just as the exterior lights blazed to life.

22

THE GUARDIANS ATTACK

Under normal circumstances, the Great Golden Mosque compound was home to a fifth of the city's nearly two hundred mech suits, as well as an additional one hundred soldiers and workers, many of which were armed with rapid-fire laser rifles. However, due to the major earthquake five days before, just over half of the normal contingent remained. The rest were on duty in other parts of the city aiding with the continual cleanup efforts.

Which is exactly why Prometheus had even agreed to an assault in the first place.

Of the twenty-four remaining mechs, the four on the southeast end had gone to apprehend Raptor and the others, and eight were on the far end on the bridges, leaving only twelve to guard the rest of the island.

Prometheus's lip curled into a twisted smile. *This is going to be fun.* He, Cerberus, and Specter had reached the central island by climbing upside down underneath the western bridge. Although they had each activated their suit's camouflage ability, making them nearly invisible to the naked eye, they knew that the mech suits and spy cameras had the capability of seeing through their disguises.

Finally, after several hours of hiding under the bridge and observing the movements of the guards, they received the call from Raptor. *We're about to have company. According to Kianna, the AAC's facial-recognition software finally located us. Are you ready?*

Prometheus let out a silent sneer. *Of course. We will start our attack as soon as Virus and your friend are in place.*

Got it. We'll hold them off until then. Good luck.

Shutting down the connection, Prometheus turned toward his two companions and sent a quick message for them to prepare, then checked in with Virus before making his own last-minute preparations.

Once all was ready, Prometheus motioned to the others. Moving as one, the three technologically enhanced Guardians slid out from concealment and launched their attack.

Raising his right arm, Prometheus used his computer targeting system to lock on to the garage door that, according to his intel, housed several military vehicles. A second later, a small compartment built into the forearm of his suit opened and unleashed its payload of six tiny rockets. Before either of the two guards at the end of the bridge even knew they were under attack, the rockets struck their target. The explosion shook the area and released a huge plume of black smoke into the air while Specter and Cerberus took down the two mechs and four foot soldiers.

Reacting to the sudden strike, the two pairs of mech guards stationed at the northwest and southwest corners spun toward the explosion. Noticing the intruders, the pilots immediately activated their suits and ran toward them.

Working in tandem, Cerberus and Specter each launched one of the EMP grenades toward the four unsuspecting opponents. The grenades released their energy, deactivating the mechs with a brilliant flash. Rushing up to the inoperable machines, the two Guardians used their heavy wrist-mounted laser weapons to tear several holes into the suits' power circuits, rendering them useless. With their mechs inoperative, the human soldiers tried frantically to get out of the suits and escape. However, with a few well-placed shots, the Guardians made sure the men were out of the battle.

First wave down, Prometheus stated through the TeleConnect. *Be ready for wave two.*

For several seconds, the enhanced humans stood in ready positions, their bodies tense and alert. Prometheus reached down and withdrew the handheld device from one of the compartments lining his belt. As expected, the Guardians' augmented hearing picked up the unmistakable clanking sounds of the two pairs of mechs stationed to the north and northeast as they made their way toward the northwest corner. At their current rate, Prometheus's internal computer calculated that they would be within firing range in four-point-nine seconds and six-point-two seconds respectively. Simultaneously, the eight mechs guarding the bridge entrances on the mainland were using their suits' hoverjets to cross the bridges, arriving at the island in eight-point-four seconds. The camera mounted at the back of his head indicated that the final two mechs from the eastern bridge were using their hoverjets to leap over the entire central courtyard and side buildings. At their current trajectory, they would land sixty-point-eight feet from where the three Guardians stood in exactly four-point-three seconds. Finally, the six regular soldiers who were unfortunate enough to be outside the buildings at the start of the attack had managed to recover from their shock, remove their rifles from their shoulder slings, and were preparing to fire.

Suddenly, the light from the dome vanished, blanketing the entire cavern in complete darkness. Having been warned seconds prior by Jade, Prometheus immediately activated the

Implant Disruptor held in his palm. The Guardians, now accustomed to the disorienting effects of the device, wasted no time in launching themselves toward their confused opponents. Prometheus and Cerberus bolted toward the northern corner of the compound. Their leg muscles, enhanced with animal DNA and cybernetic implants, covered the distance in a fraction of the time of a normal human. Meanwhile, Specter turned to face the two mechs behind him.

The pilots, caught completely off guard by the loss of the light and disoriented by the blocked implant feed, never had a chance. The three Guardians each reached their targets and had the first of the mech suits destroyed before the others could even fight off their dizziness. The robotic suits, having been designed to respond primarily to implant commands, were severely hindered without them. The second set of pilots lost several precious seconds discovering this fact, which was enough time for each of the attackers to dispose of them.

Even before the last of the four mech suits hit the ground, Prometheus and Cerberus turned to face the six plainclothes jihadist guards, who were just now recovering from the loss of their own implant feeds. Groping in the darkness, the guards were stumbling toward the still-burning garage, which was currently the only source of light. The men moved together in a small circle, their rapid-fire laser rifles pointing toward the last known location of the Guardians.

As the men drew near the blazing building, one of them shouted and pointed toward a pinprick of light that was growing larger and larger. Fear tore through the men and they scattered in all directions as realization struck them. A second later, a concussion grenade exploded in their midst, rendering them unconscious.

With a quick glance, Prometheus verified that Specter had also disposed of the soldiers near him. Scanning the area, he noticed that the two pairs of mechs that had been crossing the north and west bridges were beginning to figure out how to activate their mech suits manually without the implant commands. Prometheus looked at Cerberus and pointed to the two on the north bridge. The Hybrid nodded once, then bounded off, running on all fours, his canine fangs bared. Spinning around, Prometheus raised his right arm once more and let another rocket fly toward the western bridge. Although their movements were still a bit sluggish, the pilots managed to maneuver their mech suits far enough out of range that their armor was able to absorb the blast with minimal damage. However, Prometheus had deliberately fired the rocket a little behind them in order to force them toward the island, where they would be in range of his lasers.

The moment they stepped off the bridge, Prometheus unleashed a volley of laser fire at them. One of the men activated his suit's hoverjets and flew into the air, dodging the deadly bolts of energy. The other pilot chose to find cover behind the large beam that anchored this end of the bridge to the island.

The Guardians were part of a larger plan hatched by the governor of Elysium that included using implant technology to take over the minds of the populace. As such, the technology in their own armor was hardwired to their technological enhancements and not reliant upon implant commands. Using that advantage, Prometheus immediately launched a harmless flare, which hit the ground several feet in front of him and released a bright flash into the surrounding darkness.

Although he knew the mechs had the capability of seeing through his own suit's camouflage, he also knew that the flare would automatically darken their viewports. With precise timing, he activated his suit's camouflage and darted toward the waterfront. As expected, his actions succeeded in confusing the pilots. For several seconds, the men sprayed fire at where he had been moments before, not realizing that their prey was now closing the distance between them.

By the time their scanners detected his heat signature, Prometheus had reached the bridge. Using his enhancements, he leaped up and over the edge and landed directly on the head of the first mech. His ten-foot, four-hundred-pound bulk crushed the top portion of the suit and pinned it to the ground. The Titan let out a battle cry as he ripped large portions of wiring and armor from the top of the downed machine with his clawed hands, taking it out of the fight.

Meanwhile, his final opponent had landed and began firing wildly in an attempt to rescue his companion. Laser bolts struck the bridge, but based on the pattern of fire, Prometheus knew the pilot was fearful of hitting the other mech and wounding the pilot. Smiling, he grabbed the damaged suit in his right hand and, with a roar of exertion, lifted it in front of him to use as a shield. Inside the mech, he could hear the soldier frantically struggling to get out. Reaching around the suit with his right arm, Prometheus gave his targeting system a moment to lock on to the attacker, then sent a heat-seeking missile screaming toward the machine.

The distance between them was enough that the mech's built-in countermeasures had just enough time to fire, exploding the missile several feet prior to impact. However, the flash once again momentarily blinded the pilot as well as caused him to stumble, allowing Prometheus the brief window he needed. Tossing the damaged mech over the rail of the bridge and into the lake, he charged forward. With full implant communication, the jihadist would have been able to recover his balance, target the attacker, and fire a kill shot at the Guardian. But without the instantaneous commands, and with the pilot still unfamiliar with the manual controls, Prometheus reached him just as he was bringing his weapons to bear.

Using all of his strength and momentum, the Titan plowed into the machine and drove it into a large vehicle parked behind it. The force of the blow stunned the soldier inside the mechanical suit. Jumping back, Prometheus raised his left arm and activated another compartment in his armor. A moment later, a grenade landed under the vehicle. Coming to his senses, the pilot fought to get his mech out of the mangled vehicle. Just as he got the machine to its feet, the grenade exploded, tearing into the back of the suit.

Even before the heavily damaged mech landed face-first on the ground, Prometheus turned and began to assess the situation. All around the compound and the city proper, lights were flaring to life inside and outside the buildings. His long-range scanners tracked numerous mech units leaping into the air across the city, all headed toward the island.

Cerberus ran up beside him, his wolflike snout split in a wide grin. "Exactly as predicted. The rest of the mechs are coming to assist."

"Yes. The advantage has been lost. Time to leave. Where is Specter?"

"I don't know. The last I saw he had leapt up the side of this building and was headed toward—"

Just then, an explosion erupted from inside the courtyard, rocking the compound.

Knowing that implant communication wouldn't be possible once the operation began, Raptor had procured several commlinks and given one to each Guardian. Switching on the device, Prometheus spoke rapidly. "Specter, Virus, report."

"The final charges have been set and I'm heading for the rendezvous," came Virus's reply.

"Acknowledged. Specter?"

Prometheus and Cerberus exchanged glances at the silence that followed. With a frown, the Titan waited a few seconds more, returned the device to its compartment, then strode toward the damaged western bridge with heavy, determined strides.

Taken off guard, Cerberus had to rush to catch up. "He may still be alive!"

"That may be true. But if we wait any longer, we'll lose our escape window. We leave now. Specter is on his own."

23

TURNING TIDES

A smile crept its way across the Asian woman's face.

Jade had long ago come to terms with the routine tasks associated with her current "profession." She didn't particularly enjoy the fighting, or the stealing, or hurting people. But she justified her actions with the knowledge that she only really did it to those who were doing the same to others.

But the current situation was different. These men were the type of men who fed the slavery business. These men were just like the man who bought Catrina. These men were like the husband who had abused her for so many years. This was more than a job: this was revenge.

At least, that's what she told herself. And it was these thoughts that fueled her rage.

After shutting off the power to the Golden Dome, Jade set out to complete her second mission.

With her night vision goggles in place and her cloak stored in her backpack, Jade moved swiftly down the remaining stairs until she reached the bottom floor. Fourteen men stood around in the pitch-black darkness that enveloped the large foyer. Had the lights been on, Jade might have paused to marvel at the exquisite beauty of the room, with its gold trim, majestic columns and mosaics. But none of that mattered in the darkness. All she saw through her night vision were potential targets. She rapidly determined that eight of the men were merely other imams and posed no threat. The other six men carried weapons. *Little good it will do them,* she thought with satisfaction. After years of practice, Jade had mastered the ability to move without making even the slightest of sounds. That skill allowed her to reach her first target completely undetected. She might have been able to cross and exit the room before they were even aware of her presence, but her rage clouded her judgment. Mentally preparing herself, she launched an attack.

She jabbed her elbow into the first man's throat, causing him to gasp for air. As he did so, she spun around and landed a kick to the side of his head, knocking him unconscious. The other guard standing nearby spun around in alarm. However, confused by the sounds of the scuffle and blinded by the darkness, he merely raised his weapon.

Jade disarmed him with a kick, then pivoted in toward him, placing her right foot behind his closest leg. With a rapid strike from her right fist, she knocked the man backward. Her leg prevented him from catching himself, causing him to drop heavily to the floor. Moving into a wide stance, Jade finished him off with a solid punch to his temple.

By this time, the other men in the room began heading as rapidly as they could manage toward the three exits. Several cried out in pain as they banged into furniture or each other. To her surprise and amusement, one of the imams began crying out something in Arabic. Although she couldn't understand his words, she did catch the word *djinn,* and his terror infected the others.

Ha! The superstitious fools think I'm one of their supernatural apparitions. By the time I'm through with them, they'll have wished I was!

Taking advantage of their fear, she bolted across the room, letting out a bloodcurdling scream as she ran. The guard in front of her raised his weapon in self-defense, his expression a mask of horror.

Using her momentum, Jade lowered her shoulder and plowed into him. The man fell backward and hit his head on a nearby table, stunning him. Beside her, Jade could hear the other guard backing away as he raised his weapon. Realizing that the man's fear was overriding his sense, she threw herself on the floor as he unleashed a volley of laser fire into the darkness. The flashes of reddish light acted as a strobe, serving to enhance the man's terror. After several seconds of chaotic gunfire that destroyed nearly half of the decorations in the room and felled several of the fleeing imams, he released the trigger.

The attack was like cold water to her face, bringing her to her senses. *You're wasting time, you fool!* she chided herself. *Keep your focus on your mission.* Not wanting to expend more time with melee combat, Jade reached into her pocket, withdrew her laser pistol, and sent several shots toward the man, the last one finally connecting and dropping him to the floor.

With the laser fire having ceased, the room descended into complete darkness once more. Leaping to her feet, Jade ignored the rest of the men in the room and raced toward the far exit.

Following the map of the compound which she had memorized, she ran across the central courtyard toward the building along the northeastern side. A small amount of light from the surrounding city managed to make its way over the buildings, allowing the few people standing in the courtyard a glimpse of the fleeting shadow that flew past them.

Jade reached the far building just as lights began coming on within the buildings. Simultaneously, she heard the unmistakable sound of mech suit hoverjets. A second later, light flared in the darkness over the roof of the building behind her as two of the armored guards brought their machines to rest in the courtyard. Immediately after landing, they turned in her direction, their sensors having detected her presence.

Trapped, Jade knew she could never get the door open in time or hope to defeat two of the AAC's war machines. She frantically ran down the very short list of her options, none of which had positive outcomes.

Suddenly, a human-sized shadow detached itself from the roof of the western building and leapt toward the ten-foot-tall mechs. The pilots, reacting to their suits' alarms and warnings, spun around in a hurried attempt to mount a defense against the new threat. However, the Guardian's enhanced reflexes gave him the advantage over the clunky machines.

Jade stood in shock and relief for a few precious seconds as Specter fought against the armored guards. Finally, the lights from within the building next to her snapped her out of her daze. Letting out a curse of frustration at the loss of time, she spun around and sent several laser bolts from her gun into the lock of the nearby door. Grabbing the handle, she yanked it open.

Leading with the barrel of her pistol, she moved through several more darkened interior rooms before the lights inside the room she was in suddenly turned on, blinding her. Yanking off the goggles, she paused long enough to let her eyes adjust before continuing.

As anticipated, most of this part of the building had been deserted once the fighting had started. However, her costly delays meant that she'd have to take out any opposition in the next room without the cover of darkness. Grabbing her commlink, she activated it. "Raptor, I've reached my destination."

When no answer was forthcoming, she tried again. "Raptor, Charon, Xavier, do you hear me? I'm in position. However, it took a little longer than expected. I may need a little help over here." Again, silence. Swearing, she tucked the device away.

Typical. What's the good of having these stupid things if no one's going to answer? I guess you're on your own. Bracing herself, she removed the invisibility cloak from her backpack, wrapped it around her shoulders, and opened the door.

Seven men were moving around inside the large garage. Based on the grease stains on the hands and clothes of four of them, she guessed them to be the mechanics. The other three, however, wore the unmistakable *keffiyeh* headscarves and garb of AAC jihadists. Six heavy military vehicles were parked in bays along the left wall like giant mechanical sentinels waiting to be awakened. Twelve feet to the left from where Jade had entered, another armored truck with four sets of wheels was jacked up into the air with several large parts lying nearby on workbenches along the wall. To the right, the middle two out of the eight large garage doors stood open, each with a vehicle idling in front of it.

It became instantly clear to Jade that the mechanics were in the final stages of preparing two of the vehicles for the guards to use. Fortunately, all of the men seemed so engrossed in their activities that they failed to notice her entrance. Moving slowly so as to give her cloak's cameras time to adjust the images they projected, she worked her way around the edge of the room until she had clear shots at the guards.

The first two, who were now only twenty-five feet away from her position, never even had a chance. The third guard, however, reacting to the laser fire dove sideways behind the idling vehicle, causing her shot to miss by inches. In her peripheral vision, she saw the mechanics scattering to find cover. Recognizing that her element of surprise had passed, she was forced to rely upon her cloak's camouflage ability and her speed.

Jade darted out from her current hiding spot and ran into the nearest vehicle bay and crouched down in the shadows. As she had hoped, her quick movement allowed her to find a new hiding place before the remaining guard could recover from her initial attack. Raising her weapon, she targeted the man as he slowly peered around the front of the truck, his weapon searching for his hidden adversary.

Just as she was about to pull the trigger, she caught sight of movement to her left. Reacting instantly, she ducked just as an industrial-size wrench flew over her head to strike loudly into the parked vehicle. Still off-balance, Jade was forced to roll forward to avoid a follow-up kick from the wrench-wielding mechanic who had somehow managed to get behind her.

Coming out of her roll into a crouch, she flung the cloak back away from her face. Although it was great for stealth, the thick cloth made hand-to-hand combat much more difficult. Leaping toward the man, she dodged another clumsy attack with the wrench, then swept his feet out from under him. However, before she could finish him off, she felt strong arms wrap themselves around her from behind. Immediately, she threw her head backward, hitting the man's chin hard with the back of her head. The man's grip loosened as he fought against the sudden wave of pain, giving Jade the opening she needed to elbow him in the stomach and spin out of his grasp.

An amplified voice suddenly called out in Arabic, causing her to whirl around to search for the source. Her stomach dropped at what awaited her. Not only was she facing the barrel of the remaining guard's laser pistol, but two other guards in mech suits stood in the open garage doors, with a third mech coming up behind them. All three of the armored machines had their weapons pointed in her direction.

She had failed.

"Now what, boss?" Xavier whispered in frustration as he, Raptor, and Braedon huddled in the entryway of the building with the door at their backs. The narrow hallway they were in ended in a thick, windowless door. "In case you hadn't noticed, the lights are on!"

"We stick with the plan! As long as this baby did its job," he said in a harsh whisper as he held up the Codebreaker, "and didn't sound the back door alarm, the guards will still likely be more confused than a baby *gridik* lost in the Labyrinth just trying to figure out what's going on."

"I sure hope you're right," Xavier replied as he used his uninjured hand to lift his night vision goggles until they rested against his forehead.

"Of course I'm right," Raptor retorted as he removed his own goggles, stepped up to the security door at the other end of the short hallway, and began attaching the Codebreaker to it.

However, before he was able to complete the setup, the sound of a door opening could be heard from somewhere nearby. Jumping back, Raptor, Braedon, and Xavier stood with weapons trained on the door.

A second later, the lock clicked and the door was pushed open by a pair of guards. Although the men had weapons in their hands, the obviously surprised expressions on their faces made it clear they were not expecting to encounter any resistance inside the building. Caught off guard, the men were easily taken out of the fight by the three intruders.

With the men down, Raptor and Braedon rushed to the door to search for signs of any other attackers. The door opened into a long hallway that extended forty feet to the right and another sixty to the left. To the right, where the hallway ended, were three doors: one set into the south wall, another on the east, and another directly opposite the south door. To the left, two doors were set at even intervals into the south wall, while the opposite wall was filled with mosaics and Qur'anic verses. Suddenly, the second door along the left wall opened. Raptor's weapon immediately tracked toward the movement. However, just as he was prepared to fire, he caught sight of the terrified expressions on the faces of two lab technicians, who quickly retreated and slammed the door.

Raptor paused a moment to make sure the men hadn't alerted any guards within before he continued. "C'mon," he whispered, urging Braedon forward. Together, the two of them walked back to back down the right passage, each keeping his weapon focused on the hallway while Xavier stood nearby, his own weapon trained on each doorway they passed.

They reached the solitary door on the northern wall at the end of the east passage unchallenged. Xavier kept an eye on the rest of the hallway and Braedon focused on the two doors on the east and south wall while Raptor attached the Codebreaker to the door. Their hearts pounded painfully in their chests as adrenaline continued to pour through their bodies, making each second seem like an eternity. At last, the lock released.

"Ready? On three. One...two...three!"

Raptor kicked open the door that led to the guard room. Inside the inverted-L-shaped room were two guards standing near the lone corner bent to the left. The room had three doors along the right wall, and another door along the north wall just before the corner. The moment Braedon and Raptor entered the room, the men spun around and fumbled for their weapons. Braedon's first shot took out the guard on the right, but Raptor, thrown off-balance slightly from kicking the door, narrowly missed his target. The man reacted quickly by diving around the corner.

Frustrated by his lack of accuracy, Raptor swore and let off another round, **barely** missing the man's foot as he finished his dive. Wasting no time, Braedon ran toward the bend, reaching it in a matter of seconds. Rounding the corner, he came face-to-face with the barrel of a laser pistol. Anticipating that possibility, Braedon swatted the gun aside. The weapon discharged, its deadly energy passing harmlessly by his left ear.

With the guard's right arm extended to fire his laser pistol, Braedon took advantage of his open posture and jabbed his right elbow into the man's unprotected gut, doubling him over. A final jab with his knee ended the man's will to fight. The guard's unconscious body reached the ground right as Xavier's pistol and head peered around corner.

The con man's features relaxed noticeably at the sight of the downed guard. "Nice work. I can't believe there were only two of them. The way Raptor made it sound, there could be up to eight guards in here. Doesn't that worry you?"

Braedon frowned even as he pointed his weapon toward the closed door next to them, expecting it to open at any moment. "It's hard to tell. Prometheus's attack could have drawn them out."

"Riiiight," Xavier said. "Sorry to disagree, but my past experiences have left me a little skeptical."

He and Braedon darted back around the corner to join Raptor, who had already begun working on the locked door. Although he still wore a scowl from having missed his target, he relaxed slightly upon seeing that Braedon had cleaned up his mess. "Thanks. It seems my aim is a little off today."

"I hear that happens as you age," Xavier added, his expression one of false concern.

"You're just jealous that I'm seven years older than you *and* better looking, even with the stupid beard." Xavier opened his mouth to reply, but Raptor cut him off, returning their focus to the mission. "On the other side of the door are the cells that house important prisoners. Braedon, stay here and keep the way out secured while Xavier and I get your friends."

The light on the Codebreaker changed to green and the lock released. Nodding to Xavier, who still appeared ready for a verbal retaliation, Raptor threw the door open.

The sight that awaited him turned his blood to ice.

Before he could even react, the other four doors to the room opened, including the door from which they had just entered. Guards poured out from the adjoining rooms, each one with weapons pointed at the intruders.

Knowing they were trapped, Xavier and Braedon lifted their hands in surrender. As if turned to stone, Raptor remained frozen with his gun pointed through the doorway that led toward the cells.

"Come now, Rahib. Lower your weapon. Is this any way to greet your father?"

24

CONFRONTATION

Rahib Ahmed stared at his father, the Imam Rasul Karim Ahmed, one of the most powerful men in all of Tartarus, or *Jahannam*, as the citizens of Bab al-Jihad called it. In the nearly twenty years since he had last seen his father, he had often wondered what he would feel if he ever did see him again. Yet all of that wondering could never have prepared him for the deluge of memories and intense emotions that assailed him in that single moment.

He remembered feelings of excitement, pride, and accomplishment from his childhood as he studied the Qur'an in the mosque under the tutelage of his father and the other imams. He remembered times of laughter and mischief that he had shared with his younger sister. He remembered feelings of confusion and conflict as well as he moved into his early teenage years.

But, most of all, he also remembered the feelings of betrayal, anger, hatred, and fear. And with the feelings came the memories that he had buried deep in his subconscious since leaving home all those years ago.

Raptor narrowed his eyes and tightened his grip on his laser pistol. For a brief second, he warred within himself against the desire to pull the trigger and end his father's life right here and now as payback for the pain the man had inflicted on him. He didn't care if it meant the guards would kill him. At least he would have justice.

As his finger tightened on the trigger, he felt something stay his hand. Some voice within his spirit kept him from following through. In that moment of hesitation, one of the guards reached up and took away his pistol, and his one chance to murder his father.

Numb, Raptor could only watch as his father stepped toward him. He had aged greatly over the years. Although he still kept his beard short and neatly trimmed, streaks of gray now ran through the dark hair. And, from what he could see sticking out from around the edges of the solid white *taqiyah* cap, his hair was thinning. Despite these outer changes, Raptor could tell by the arrogant stance, proud posture, and inner fire fueling his eyes that his father hadn't changed.

"My son—"

"Don't call me that!" Raptor spat out, interrupting him. "I stopped being your son when I left this city."

A flicker of pain crossed his face but was quickly swept away. "Yet here you are. I must say, the beard suits you."

Raptor reached up and yanked the false beard and cap off his head, just to spite the man.

"Hm…While the beard made you look older and more distinguished, the short, neatly trimmed beard does suit you. You have grown into quite a handsome young man. I see myself in your eyes. You can't deny your heritage. Although you may not want to accept it, Allah placed within you a deep desire to return home."

"Think what you want, old man. I'm not here to stay."

"Ah, yes," the imam said, switching over to English. Turning, he nodded at two of the guards before returning his gaze to his son. "You're here to rescue your friends. Although, I must admit, based on the reports I heard, these two don't exactly fit the mold of your normal choice of companions."

For the first time, Raptor noticed the other men standing behind the imam. To his father's left, as always, was his top commander and advisor, Taj El-Mofty. As always, the expression of the man's face teetered between smugness and self-righteous snobbery. Behind him, four jihadist militants were spread out, their posture tense and alert. Between the two in the middle stood an older man with gray hair, and a balding middle-aged man.

"Gunther! Travis!"

Looking over his shoulder toward the speaker, Raptor suddenly remembered for the first time since his father's appearance that Braedon and Xavier were here with him, both men bound with their hands behind their backs. Turning back around, he saw Gunther frown. "Braedon? Is that you?"

Braedon nodded and offered a weak smile. Gunther tried to smile in return, but his countenance fell. Unable to hold Braedon's gaze, he lowered his head and resumed his staring contest with the floor of the room. The old man's shoulders drooped, and Raptor could see defeat and resignation on his face.

"Yes, your friends are in good health," the imam continued. "Even though they are infidels, Allah has chosen them to be his instruments."

"Instruments for what?" Raptor couldn't help but ask.

"To bring you back to me. To open the way back to earth. To punish the infidels who oppose us. And, to usher in the return of the Mahdi. The Twelfth Imam. The Messiah!"

Slowly, the realization of what his father believed and planned worked its way through Raptor's mind like a poison. "You're delusional! You think *you* are the Twelfth Imam!"

"Yes! Why not?" the imam asked as he drew near to Raptor, his eyes ablaze with holy zeal. "Does not tradition teach that the Mahdi is to be born then disappear and be hidden from humanity for a time before reappearing again to bring justice to the world? I was born on earth, but only arrived in Jahannam as a little child. I will return again and bring my army with me! I will lead the faithful from this prison into the light, and we will conquer and bring peace to the world of our birth!"

Raptor suddenly felt sick as another thought occurred to him. "And what of the rest of the population of Tartarus? What will become of them?"

The imam's face hardened. "They will convert to Islam, or face Allah's judgment."

"And what is that? Are you going to just leave them here?"

"Why? So they can continue to wallow in sin and pervert life to create their abominations? No. Once we have evacuated the faithful to earth, we will unleash a toxin into the caverns of all of Jahannam that will eventually wipe them out."

"No...," Braedon said softly as the truth sank in. "You'll murder millions of innocent people!"

"They are not innocent!" the imam railed as he turned his attention toward his prisoner. "They have willfully rejected Allah and his prophet, peace be unto him. It is our duty to wage jihad on them and purge them from the world. Yes. Allah is indeed smiling upon me. Can you not see how he has orchestrated events to bring us to this moment?

"First, he allowed these infidels to discover the means of our salvation," he continued, gesturing toward Gunther and Travis. "Then, he placed one of my men in the right place at the right time to overhear your foolish friend Xavier give the details about your operation in Dehali during one of his late-night *Pandora's Box* sessions."

"What?" Raptor asked, his head whipping around to stare at Xavier. "*That's* how they knew where we were? You told me you wouldn't get hooked on any more *Box* sessions."

Xavier grimaced. "I'm...I'm sorry! I tried! How was I supposed to know they were listening?"

"You see, my son, you cannot escape the will of Allah," the imam continued. "By capturing these men, the only thing we still lacked was the machine they created. Now, he has not only brought the machine to Bab al-Jihad, but he has also returned my son to me."

Raptor let out a curse.

"I am impressed," he said, ignoring the outburst. "We knew you were in the city, but you have been clever in staying hidden. Then, with your sister's help, we finally had your location. Yet, somehow you found out about the tracker and eluded us again. In hindsight, I'm sure the abominations from Elysium had something to do with that. We knew you would try to rescue your friends, but we never anticipated the attack from the Guardians. I will admit, they are quite formidable. You will have to share with me how you managed to get them to cooperate with you, and how you managed this neat trick of blocking all implant communication. That one in particular has my generals quite upset. In fact, I'm going to have to insist you to cease blocking the signals now."

"I wouldn't even if I could. I don't have control over that. The Guardians have the device," Raptor said with a sneer.

Imam Ahmed frowned. "I see. How convenient. It won't make a difference. Once we have retrieved the Vortex weapon from your other friends, the implants here will be pointless." He paused, noticing the slight twitch in Raptor's composure. "Yes, son. Your friend was quite good at hacking into our system. My technicians tell me she is one of the best they ever encountered. However, she finally made a mistake that allowed my men to trace her signal. Even now, a team of soldiers is on their way to her location. In fact, they may already have her in custody."

"No!" Braedon called out in shock. "Catrina!"

"Yes, I had almost forgotten about Zarrar's wife, and his murderer! Taj, bring him here to me."

Taj El-Mofty stepped forward without hesitation, grabbed Braedon from behind, and shoved him roughly forward. When they were within a foot of the imam, El-Mofty forced his prisoner to his knees.

"I've heard about you," the imam said, leaning over Braedon. "You are the *Christian* that has been traveling with my son, no doubt trying to poison him and turn him away from the truth."

Standing next to Braedon, Raptor sneered. "He didn't need to. You did that all by yourself."

The imam ignored Raptor once again. Without taking his gaze from Braedon, he called out a command to his general. "Bring me a sword."

Taj El-Mofty let a slight grin twist his lip before nodding, then exited the room.

"Wait a second," Raptor said, a sudden urgency in his voice. He felt his gut twist painfully at the thought of what was coming. "Don't do this!"

The imam raised an eyebrow and turned his attention toward Raptor. "What is this? Why would you defend this infidel? Am I too late? Has he already poisoned your mind? Tell me, Rahib? Have you truly turned your back on Allah and accepted this... this man's heresy? You know the blasphemy these Christians teach! They claim that Allah took physical form to impregnate Mary, the mother of Isha!" The imam's voice began rising in volume, as if he were now addressing a congregation. Indeed, all of the guards in the room stood enraptured by their leader's words.

"They claim he is the *son* of Allah! But the holy Qur'an says, 'the Messiah, Jesus, son of Mary, was nothing more than a messenger of God, his word, directed to Mary, a spirit from him. So believe in God and his messengers and do not speak of a

"Trinity"—stop, that is better for you—God is only one God, he is far above having a son, everything in the heavens and earth belongs to him and he is the best one to trust.'[1]

"And later, it says in Sura 5, 'If anyone associates others with God, God will forbid him from the Garden, and Hell will be his home. No one will help such evildoers. Those people who say that God is the third of three are defying the truth: there is only One God. If they persist in what they are saying, a painful punishment will afflict those of them who persist.'[2]"

"That's not true," Braedon said softly. "That's not what we believe."

The imam backhanded his prisoner, the force of the blow knocking Braedon to the floor. "You are an infidel and a deceiver!" As he finished speaking, Taj El-Mofty reentered the room carrying a terrifyingly beautiful sword, adorned with Arabic letters and designs.

"Father, this isn't right!" Raptor stated, his frustration and anger rising. "There should be no compulsion in religion!"

"Do *not* presume to know the words of Allah better than I!" Grabbing the sword from El-Mofty's hand, he nodded toward the guards behind Braedon. The two jihadist militants held their prisoner down, leaving the back of his neck exposed. "Bring the other one also!"

"What?" Xavier cried out in panic. "I'm not…wait!" One of the guards hit Xavier on the side of his head to quiet him, then he and his partner dragged their prisoner forward, forcing him to kneel beside Braedon.

"I am not without mercy," the imam stated. "I will give them a chance to accept the truth. Do you renounce your false beliefs and recognize the truth? Speak the words of the *Shahada* three times and I will spare your life. 'I bear witness that there is no god but Allah, and I bear witness that Muhammad is the messenger of Allah.'"

Gunther and Travis stared helplessly at the plight of their friends, while Raptor's face reddened with rage. Beside him, Xavier trembled in terror. "I...I will...I'll say it! Please...just don't...I...I bear witness that there is no god but...Allah, and I... um...bear witness that Muhammad is...the messenger of Allah!"

After he repeated it twice more, a mixed expression of surprise, disappointment, and exaltation crossed the imam's face. "Yes, your friend is wise. He has chosen the path of truth! Now, what about you, *Christian?*"

Raptor looked toward Braedon and was shocked by the look of peace on the man's face. "Raptor, remember your promise. Take care of Catrina for me."

"No!" Raptor shouted, struggling against the guards who held him.

Imam Ahmed raised his sword. "Speak the words, infidel! Renounce your false beliefs and live! You and your wife may yet be spared!"

Braedon looked up at the imam, tears streaming down his face. "I could never renounce my Savior, my King! Jesus is the Son of the Almighty God. He is the King of kings and Lord of lords. There is no other name under heaven given to mankind by which we must be saved!"

The imam's face turned bright red as religious zeal sent adrenaline coursing through his veins and added strength to his arms. "You see!" he shouted. "By your own words of blasphemy you condemn yourself! Now, receive the punishment for your sin!"

1. Sura 4:171
2. Sura 5:72-75

25

UNINTENDED CONSEQUENCES

The sudden loud, metallic grating sound of the door locks sliding into place halted Imam Ahmed's killing stroke. He and his men all stared around in alarm as several of them ran to the various doors scattered around the room and tried unsuccessfully to open them.

"Imam, someone has activated the—"

But before Taj El-Mofty could finish his sentence, gas began pouring into the room through the ventilation system. Despite their best efforts to ward off the gas, everyone in the room began gagging and coughing uncontrollably.

"No...," the imam managed weakly before falling to his knees. As he felt the inevitable pull of unconsciousness drag him down, he managed one last look at his son before collapsing to the ground.

Within seconds, all movement in the room ceased.

"Rahib..." The voice was gentle, yet the urgency in it gave him the extra will he needed to fight off the remaining effects of the gas and return to consciousness.

"Wha...who's there?"

"Rahib, you have to wake up! We don't have much time!"

He opened his eyes and spent several seconds trying to focus on the face of the person crouching in front of him. Finally, the synapses in his brain managed to make the necessary connection. As the identity of the person registered in his mind, he jolted up into a sitting position. Although he immediately regretted the sudden movement, he felt his heart pound heavily in his chest as the memories came flooding back.

"Zahra! You're...you're here. What...what happened?" Even as he forced the words through his lips, he stared around at the unconscious forms of his father, Braedon, and all the others who had been locked in the room. In addition to his sister, three other men who had arrived with her were already beginning to attend to Braedon, Xavier, Gunther, and Travis.

Zahra put an arm around her brother to steady him. "I...I told my husband about what you intended to do."

"You...you did what?"

"You must understand, Rahib, that not all of us agree with our father's teachings. When I told Shafiq everything, he knew that we had to help you."

"Then why did you give me the Qur'an if you knew it had a tracker on it?"

"Because our father *made* me!" Zahra said, a pleading look in her beautiful eyes. "I had to do it, or he would have suspected."

Raptor, still dazed, noticed that Braedon and the others were beginning to stir. Noticing as well, Zahra put her *hijab* in place once more, covering all but her eyes. "I wish you had trusted me. It would have made things much easier. Since we didn't know when you'd attempt the rescue, we had to come up with reasons to remain nearby. Once we heard the first explosion, we moved as quickly as we could to get here, but the loss of light from the Dome made it so difficult, we almost didn't make it in time."

"But, how did you…how did you lock the doors and pump the gas into the room?" Raptor asked, his thoughts beginning to clear. Next to him, he couldn't help but stare at the comatose form of his father, the sword still clenched in his hand.

"Shafiq was once part of Father's inner circle," Zahra said as she helped Raptor to his feet. "He knew that the door locks and gas were part of the security system to prevent any prisoners from escaping. We came through the front, surprised the guards, and checked the cameras. As soon as we saw what was happening, we immediately activated the gas."

"When this is over, you know the guards will tell the imam who it was that did all this," Raptor said, shaking his head. "You've put yourselves in serious danger!"

"No, we haven't," one of the men said as he left Xavier's side and stepped toward them. He wore the long, embroidered *kurta* shirt that came to his knees and matching pants that was common among Muslim men. His beard was gray and thick, but well maintained. "When we entered the building, we pretended we were running from attackers. We then set off a flash bomb and stunned the guards. We've given each of them a little something that causes short-term memory loss. When they awaken, they won't remember anything from the last hour."

"Rahib, this is my husband, Shafiq."

Raptor shook his hand and studied the man. Although he appeared many years older than Zahra, his eyes lacked the hardness that he saw in so many others. Had circumstances been different, Raptor felt this man was someone he might have respected. In fact, considering that his sister spoke well of him, and since he had just risked his life to rescue them, Raptor knew he already *did* respect him.

"*Asalaam Alaykum,*" Raptor said, offering the traditional greeting. "We are in your debt. Thank you."

"*Wa 'Alaykum Asalaam,*" Shafiq responded. Switching to English, he said, "If all that you told Zahra is true, then all of Tartarus may soon be in *your* debt. Is it true? Have these men created a device that can reverse the portals to earth?"

By this time, the other two men had awakened the others. At Shafiq's comment, the three of them turned toward Gunther and Travis, who were having a conversation with one of the other men.

Ignoring the looks from Raptor, Zahra, and Shafiq, Gunther ceased his conversation and stood slowly. Once he had gained his balance, he strode over to Braedon and embraced him, weeping as he did so.

"Thank God you're alive!" he said, his words muffled by Braedon's shoulder. "I thought...I can't imagine..."

"Yes," Braedon whispered, his own tears spilling down his cheeks once more. "Thank God."

Gaining a bit more control of his emotions, Gunther pulled back and held his friend at arm's length. "You came for us! I...I'm so...thankful. Gorbat said you were in the city, but...Oh, I forgot. Braedon, I'd like you to meet Gorbat," he said, turning to look at the man who was even now helping Travis stand.

Raptor cleared his throat loudly to interrupt. "Gunther, Travis, it's good to see you're both doing well. I'm afraid the introductions will have to be cut short. Right now we've got to get out of here."

Travis shook his head, his expression turning to intense concern and worry. "We can't! My...my family is still here somewhere. We can't leave without them!"

"Who told you they were here?" Zahra asked.

"Taj El-Mofty. He told Gunther and me that if we didn't work on the device they would..." Unable to give voice to the horrible things that might happen to his family, he let the sentence go unfinished.

Shafiq placed a hand on Travis's shoulder. "Rest easy. I can assure you that your family isn't here. Taj has been known to lie to prisoners in order to get them to comply."

Travis didn't look convinced. "But what if you're wrong? I can't take that chance!"

"I understand your concern, but you need to trust my information. I have many sources. In fact, I can tell you that I've even seen some communications from spies who are in Dehali specifically looking for your family! They have notified the imam that they've still been unable to find them."

Braedon gave him a sympathetic look. "Look, Travis, even if they *are* here, we have no idea where they are or how to get to them. And, all of Tartarus, including your family, may die if we don't reverse the portals. We have to go!"

Still concerned but recognizing the truth of the situation, Travis nodded his assent.

"You *can* reverse the portals, right?" Raptor asked, desperately hoping for confirmation.

The two scientists exchanged glances before Gunther finally replied. "Yes, we believe so. The data we recorded from the portal opening in Dehali gave us the information we needed to calibrate the Vortex weapon. But…it can only be done at a location where the portals appear, and we need the weapon. Where is it? Didn't the imam say he had some soldiers on the way to capture it?"

Raptor swore loudly. "Yes, he did. We've got to warn Kianna." He quickly grabbed his commlink and activated it. "Kianna! Kianna can you hear me?"

"Yes! Raptor, what's going on? I'm hearing all sorts of—"

"Kianna, listen. You've got to—" His sentence was cut off by a high-pitched shrill of feedback that came through the speaker. Raptor cast a concerned look at Braedon. "Something's disrupting the signal."

"Oh, no...," Gunther said, his face going suddenly ashen.

"What?" Braedon said, his anxiety spiking. "What's wrong?"

"If they send guards after her, do you...do you think she'll try to use the Vortex against them, like I did against the Chimera Guardian back in Elysium?"

Raptor and Braedon exchanged glances. "Probably. We mentioned that as an option if she and Cat were somehow threatened. Why? What's wrong?"

For a moment, Gunther and Travis both looked sick, as if they might pass out once more. Finally, Travis broke the heavy silence. "Because, we...we finally discovered the reason for the earthquakes and instability that Tartarus has been experiencing lately."

Gunther swallowed heavily. "The Vortex was never designed as a weapon! Until it's calibrated, it's dangerous. If you remember, the first major earthquakes didn't start appearing until after I fired the weapon in Elysium."

Raptor's eyes narrowed. "What exactly are you saying?"

"I'm saying that if Kianna uses it again, it could cause more instability! We believe the Vortex is the cause! It may have formed a breach in time and space that could eventually rip all of Tartarus apart!"

"Kianna! Kianna can you hear me?"

At the sound of his voice, Kianna was both instantly relieved and concerned by the urgency of his tone. "Yes! Raptor, what's going on? I'm hearing all sorts of—"

Her words morphed into a scream as compressed waves of sound hit the Spelunker. She fell to the floor of the vehicle and curled into a ball, desperately attempting to fight against the sudden nausea. Then, just as suddenly as it had started, the attack ceased.

As her head cleared, she slowly regained her strength. Glancing in the backseat, she noticed with relief that Catrina appeared to still be breathing, despite the intensity of the sound waves. *They must've been trying to knock us out quickly. The only reason I'm still conscious is because I happened to be wearing noise-cancelling earbuds! If I hadn't been listening in on the military implant feeds from the city, I would have...* She let the thought go unfinished.

Slowly raising her head, she peered through the front windshield of the Spelunker. Her pulse quickened at the sight of the two mechs and four guards that were standing not more than forty feet away. Thankful that Raptor had picked a hiding place next to the cavern wall where a potential threat could only approach from the front, Kianna quickly ran through her options. Quickly realizing that ramming two mechs would accomplish nothing, she reached under the seat for her only hope.

Her hands shook as she unzipped the bag and withdrew the large device. Raptor and Braedon had explained to her how to use it and had warned her about what to expect and what *not* to do. Fear seized her in its cold grip, threatening to incapacitate her. Hurried prayers fell from her lips as she crawled toward the side door. "God...please...help me!" Taking a deep breath, she flung open the door, raised the weapon, and pulled the trigger.

Despite the warnings and preparations that Raptor and Braedon had given her, nothing could have prepared her for what happened. The sound of rushing wind filled the air as a narrow cone of purplish particles flew out of the nozzle of the rifle-like weapon, heading straight for the soldiers. Confronted by the strange sight, the men turn and fled down the narrow street toward where the mechs waited. The pilots of the ten-foot-tall machines stood their ground and opened fire with their sound compressors once again.

As the waves pummeled her, Kianna cried out once more and fell backward onto the street. However, the adrenaline in her body kept her finger on the trigger even as the Vortex tilted upward at a forty-five-degree angle. Just as the weapon had finished making the smaller, four-foot-wide ring of particles, it shot them outward at the new angle. The end result was that instead of opening the miniature black hole several dozen feet in front of her, it opened it fifteen feet from the ground, just over the heads of the mechs.

The sight of the beautiful yet horrible tear in space caused the mech pilots to cease their attack on Kianna. With the pressure gone, she managed to retain enough sense to release the trigger. But the damage was done.

Crying out in terror, the four regular soldiers scrambled to escape from the pull of the swirling ring of death. However, within seconds, the men disappeared into nothingness. The mech pilots, caught off guard by the sudden pull on their machines, tried activating their hoverjets. With a sickening crash of metal on metal, the two mechs collided in midair as the gravitational forces confused their sensors. Trapped in their metal prisons, the pilots watched helplessly as the hungry energy force pulled them to their doom.

Although she was farther away from the eye of the maelstrom, Kianna let out a cry as she felt herself being dragged slowly down the street as the black hole increased in power. Frantic, she looked for something to grab on to. With the engine off, the hover technology that kept the Spelunker aloft was deactivated, causing the vehicle to rest on its four metal parking legs. Spying a small gap in a section of one of the front legs, she reached out with the Vortex and wedged the weapon into the gap.

Dazed, nauseated, and terrified beyond reason, Kianna held on with all her strength. Tears ran down her flushed cheeks as she cried out from exertion. Finally, just when she felt she couldn't hold on another moment, she heard another loud whoosh of air as the black hole collapsed. Released from the grip of the gravitational forces, Kianna let go of the weapon and wept.

26

THE BEGINNING OF THE END

Jade winced in pain as the mechanic twisted her arms tightly behind her back and pushed her toward the guard. As they drew nearer, the Arab man's features hardened and a wicked smile spread across his face. "I see fire in your eyes," he said in English, his accent thick and heavy. Grabbing her jaw in his right hand, he turned her head from side to side. "I don't know where you come from, or why you are here, but perhaps the imam will grant me rights of conquest. Yes, you will make an excellent prize."

"I'd rather die first!" With rage pumping energy into her muscles, she spat in the man's face and, leaning back into the mechanic holding her, lifted her feet off the ground and planted them squarely into the man's abdomen. Bringing her feet back down, she used her momentum to lean forward. Caught off guard, the mechanic still managed to hold on to her, but lost his balance. Using that to her advantage, she twisted to the side and managed to get one of her arms free from his grasp. Spinning so that her still-captured wrist was now comfortably in front of her, she stepped in toward the man, jabbed her elbow into his chin, twisted again, and yanked her arm down toward where his thumb held her. Unable to take the force, his thumb released its grip. She kicked the man twice, then spun around to finish off the guard, who had just regained his footing. With fury born of desperation and deep inner wounding, Jade kicked the man multiple times until he stopped moving.

Only then did she see the mech pilots raising their weapons to attack. After what she had just done to their comrades, she knew they would not take her prisoner. Letting out a feral cry fueled by both rage and fear of her impending death, she braced herself for the end.

However, to her absolute amazement and surprise, the third mech that stood behind the pair in the front unleashed a barrage of blaster fire into the other two. Within seconds, the attack had reduced the war machines into smoking heaps of metal. Then, just to make sure the pilots wouldn't cause any more trouble, the pilot of the third mech activated the machine's compressor, sending waves of disabling sound washing over the now-inert mechs.

Jade stood completely still in stunned disbelief as her rescuer finally addressed her using the mech's voice amplifier. "Well, this is a first. I can't remember a time when you've looked this helpless and shocked. I'm kind of surprised, considering you're the one who called me saying you could use some help."

"Charon, you idiot! What took you so long? I could've been killed!" Jade yelled, all of her pent-up emotion and adrenaline exploding at once.

"Wow. Such gratitude. And to think I figured you'd be *happy* to see me."

"Where'd you get that thing, anyway?"

"Long story," Charon replied. "It took me awhile to figure out how to run the stupid thing, especially since all of the labels are in Arabic. But I think I've got the basics down now. If you're nice to me, I may even let you try it sometime."

Despite her best efforts, a slow grin spread across her Asian features. "I don't know. You're asking an awful lot. We'll talk about it later. Let's get moving before someone takes interest in your handiwork."

Grabbing her gun and cloak, which had fallen off in the scuffle, she headed off toward the driver's door of the idling military truck. She had barely taken two steps when a loud boom filled the air, followed abruptly by a complete power outage. The only source of light anywhere in the garage came from the small running lights from Charon's mech.

"Well, it looks like our last little surprise of the day has arrived," Charon commented, this time choosing to use their commlinks rather than the mech's voice amplifier. "Better late than never. At least Virus did his job. I was wondering whether he stood us up or couldn't get the job done."

"It would've been nice if it had been on schedule. At least it was in time to help us escape. Speaking of which, let's get going." Reaching into her pack, she found her goggles, placed them back over her eyes, and headed off toward the driver's side door of the idling vehicle.

Once she was safely inside the cab of the military truck, she activated her commlink. "Raptor, I've secured our ride. Are you ready for pickup?"

After several tense seconds, she felt her stress drop another notch as Raptor responded. "Yes. We've got Gunther and Travis. Change of plans. With the power outage, we'll just meet you at the front."

"Got it. By the way, what happened to you? I tried the comm earlier and you didn't respond."

"No time for explanations. We've got to get to the Spelunker. The imam sent some of his men after the Vortex!"

Jade swore and hit the accelerator, forcing the lumbering beast into motion. "We'll be there in less than a minute. Be ready."

"We?"

"Yeah. Charon decided to show up."

"Good," Raptor said with a sigh. "I was wondering what had happened to him."

"We're on our way."

Shutting off the comm, Jade turned down the main roadway that encircled the island. As they had planned, the loss of the main power generator to the island crippled most activity. With nearly all remaining mech units either making their way *to* the island or looking for the recently disappeared Guardians, her stolen truck moved about unchallenged. Due to the loss of the implant feeds and loss of power, all of the foot soldiers and guards were left without any guidance or organization. Most just chose to stay at their posts, with only a few stumbling in the dark toward various buildings to relay messages.

However, she did notice with satisfaction that a number of vehicles were starting to come to life as some of the nonmilitary personnel decided that fleeing the island was suddenly a better option than sticking around for whatever might come next.

Jade pulled up at the semicircular driveway that ran in front of the building where the others waited, the automatic headlights of the truck cutting a path through the darkness. Glancing at her rear camera display, she noticed that Charon's lone mech followed close behind, its own headlamps blazing. Fortunately, Charon had enough sense to continue walking the grounds as if patrolling the area to search for targets.

"You'd better make this quick," Charon's voice came through the commlink. "I've had a few of these nutjobs come up and try talking to me. I just ignored them, but sooner or later someone might wonder why."

"Just keep up the ruse for a little longer. Raptor and the others are coming out right now. In fact, why don't you move on ahead toward the bridge. We'll catch up. It might look suspicious if you're with us. Unless, of course, you'd rather ditch your new toy and hop aboard."

Charon harrumphed loudly. "Not a chance! Besides, this thing might really come in handy in the future. All right, I'll catch up with you guys later."

Jade watched the lone mech move into a run for several moments before the sound of the truck's doors opening drew her attention. "It's good to see you," she said as Raptor climbed into the front seat.

"Yeah, you too."

She was going to comment on the brevity of his reply, but after taking one look at his face, realized that he was clearly not in the mood for small talk. Once everyone was on board, they closed the doors of the truck and headed toward the bridge.

As soon as they began moving, Jade heard Braedon's voice coming from the backseat. "Kianna, Kianna, are you there? Please respond."

Jade was about to ask Raptor for more details when a weary voice filled with sorrow and grief responded to Braedon's call.

"Braedon...They're...they're all dead. I...I did what you said and...I used the Vortex. Oh God, please forgive me!"

Gunther placed his hand over his mouth and Travis's eyes grew wide. Braedon's eyes closed as he offered up a quick prayer before responding. "You did the right thing. If you hadn't done that, you and Cat would've been captured, and the imam would have the weapon now. Listen to me, Kianna. You know this isn't just about us. Keep that in mind. All of Tartarus will collapse if we can't reverse the portals. Everyone, including Alayna and your parents are counting on us."

There was a long pause before Kianna's voice returned. "You're right. It's just...I keep hearing their screams..."

"Kianna, this is Raptor. Where are you now? How long ago did it happen?"

"The...black hole thing just vanished a few minutes before I picked up the comm. We're still...we're still at your hiding spot."

"You've got to get moving! Some of the AAC soldiers are sure to have seen what happened. They're probably already heading toward your location. Get out of the city. Use the western exit. Three miles into the tunnel there's a small alcove that splits off from the main tunnel. Go into that alcove, shut off all the lights, and wait for us there. Do you understand? Don't stop for anyone. We're about ten minutes behind you."

"I...I understand. Please hurry."

"Keep the comm on. If you need us, we're right here," Braedon said with concern.

"Thank you."

Braedon closed down the comm and leaned over, his head in his hands. Sitting in the back of the truck, Gunther and Travis began whispering rapidly. Seeing that something was obviously disturbing the two scientists, Raptor called out to them. "What is it?"

The men ceased their conversation immediately and turned to Raptor. When Travis replied, his tone was low and filled with an unmistakable dread. "We've got to get out of this city! If she activated the Vortex, the tear in time and space will become larger!"

"How much time do we have?" Raptor asked.

"Who knows?" Gunther replied. "From the time I activated the Vortex in Elysium to the first earthquake was nearly a week."

"But we know that the *svith* were fleeing from their homes before that," Travis countered. "You told me you ran into a group of them about a day's drive from Dehali, right?"

"Yes," Gunther nodded. "The truth is, we have no way of knowing. It could be days, hours, or even minutes before we begin to see the impact."

"But one thing we can be sure of," Travis added, his face grim, "Tartarus doesn't have much time. This is the beginning of the end."

AFTERWORD

Why do we believe what some people say, but not others? It usually is a question of authority. We often trust what someone says because they appear to be an authority on the issue. One definition of authority from the dictionary is "an expert on a subject." That expertise comes in two forms: knowledge and ability.

We live in a society that has set rules and regulations in place to make sure that those who are in positions of authority have earned the right to that title. For example, doctors, lawyers, teachers, pilots, etc., must all have certificates or degrees. This gives the average person a sense of security knowing that the person has achieved a set standard of knowledge and ability in a particular area.

And yet, when it comes to religion, many people too often live on blind faith. As I've mentioned in Bab al-Jihad, it is important to examine the founder of the religion. Why should we trust his authority? Where did he get his knowledge from, and did he demonstrate any abilities or experience that would make us trust his word?

In these author's notes, I want to summarize several of the major "monotheistic" religions and ask that you carefully consider the question of authority.

ISLAM

Founder: Muhammad

When founded: Early 7th Century

Age of founder at the time: 40

Source of authority: Claimed to have been visited by the angel Gabriel and given the Qur'an over a 23-year period

Scriptures: Qur'an; Hadith (collections of things Muhammad and companions did and said)

Who is Jesus? Another prophet of Allah. In Islam, he never died on the cross. Someone, perhaps Judas, was made to look like Jesus and took his place.

Salvation: Through works, especially by following the Five Pillars of Islam:

1) Confession (*shahada*)
2) Prayer (*salat*)
3) Giving (*zakat*)
4) Fasting during Ramadan (*sawm*)
5) Pilgrimage to Mecca (*hajj*)

MORMONISM (LATTER-DAY SAINTS)

Founder: Joseph Smith

When founded: 1820s

Age of founder at the time: Between 14 to 24 years

Source of authority: Claimed to have been visited by God the Father, Jesus, and the angel Moroni. Received golden plates, which only he could translate. The plates were eventually lost.

Scriptures: Book of Mormon; the Doctrine and Covenants; the Pearl of Great Price; the Bible ("only as it is translated correctly;" Joseph Smith began his own "inspired" translation)

Who is Jesus? The firstborn of all of God's spirit children. Lucifer and Jesus are spirit brothers, and we are all their siblings.

Salvation: Through works by following all the laws and ordinances of the church.

JEHOVAH'S WITNESSES

Founder: Charles Taze Russell

When founded: 1880s

Age of founder at the time: 18–29

Source of authority: Charles T. Russell's teachings

Scriptures: New World Translation (NWT) of the Bible (translated by Jehovah's Witnesses and changed to conform to *Watchtower* teachings); the *Watchtower* magazine

Who is Jesus? Michael the archangel; as such, he was a created being

Salvation: Through works by following the teachings of the *Watchtower*

JUDAISM (ORTHODOX)

Founder: Multiple authors of the Old Testament

When founded: During the Exodus from Egypt

Age of founder at the time: N/A

Source of authority: Claim of divine inspiration to multiple people who wrote 39 books

Scriptures: The Torah (first five books of the Old Testament), the Tanakh (the rest of the Old Testament), the Talmud (the teachings of the Jewish rabbis)

Who is Jesus? A controversial Jewish teacher (some called him a prophet), not the Messiah.

Salvation: Through works and being descendents of Abraham

CHRISTIANITY

Founder: Multiple authors of the Old *and* New Testaments, and on the historical death and resurrection of Jesus Christ

When founded: 1st century between 30–70 AD/CE

Age of founder at the time: Jesus was 30–33 years old during his public ministry

Source of authority: Claims of divine inspiration to multiple authors who wrote 66 books

Scriptures: The Bible (both the Old and New Testaments)

Who is Jesus? The Messiah of the Jewish tradition, and the second person of the Trinity

Salvation: Through grace alone, by repenting of one's sins and trusting in Jesus Christ as Savior. Salvation is purely a gift from God.

NOTE: *The above information is just a summary. The beliefs of each of these religions are multifaceted and contain complex nuances.*

Do you see a pattern? Islam, Latter-Day Saints, and Jehovah's Witnesses ALL teach that traditional Christianity was
corrupt and that their founder corrected the errors from the
Bible. On what do each of these men base their authority? Two
of the three base it on angelic visitations given to one man, and
the third is simply the teachings of one man.

Anyone can claim knowledge, but how would one verify
that knowledge, especially with religion? Religious teachings
alone cannot be verified, except perhaps by behavioral studies.
However, knowledge can be critiqued by logic. Is the religion
coherent? Does it contradict itself? Did the founder's life contradict his teachings?

In regards to the religious founder's ability, that can only
be demonstrated by prophecy or miracles. From my research, I
am not aware of any of the founders of any other religion giving accurate prophecies or performing miracles, except Jesus
and the disciples. In fact, although the Qur'an teaches that
Muhammad was a greater prophet than Jesus, it acknowledges
that Jesus performed miracles, yet Muhammad did not. "And
We gave unto Jesus, son of Mary, clear miracles" (Qur'an 2:87).
How is it that founders of these religions believe that the proph-
ets of the Old Testament were given power by God to perform
miracles to prove their authority, yet God didn't give the founders of these religions the ability to perform miracles to prove
their authority?

What knowledge or ability did Muhammad present? What
miracles did Joseph Smith perform? What prophecies did
Charles T. Russell speak? None! In fact, the Watchtower Society
has given numerous prophecies over the years that have clearly
been proven false.

In stark contrast, Christianity, which is a fulfillment of the
Jewish Old Testament, is based on multiple eyewitness accounts
of historical events. Furthermore, Jesus proved his authority by

not only speaking numerous prophecies that were fulfilled, but also by performing many miracles (not the least of which was rising from the dead!). His disciples, many of whom wrote portions of the New Testament, were not only eyewitness of his miracles, but also performed many themselves, as recorded in the book of Acts.

Can we "prove," scientifically, that one religion is correct and the others false? No. But, I do believe we can make a logical, rational decision regarding whose authority we should trust. Will you place your trust in one person who received a private revelation that is unverifiable, or will you place your trust in multiple people who were all witnesses of public events that are historically verifiable through archeology and other written documents?

Finally, every major religion of the world has to answer the question: Who was (and is) Jesus Christ? Was he Michael the archangel? An "enlightened" man? Only a prophet? Or the Son of God? The famous Christian apologist C. S. Lewis had this to say in his book, *Mere Christianity*:

> I am trying here to prevent anyone saying the really foolish thing that people often say about Him: I'm ready to accept Jesus as a great moral teacher, but I don't accept his claim to be God. That is the one thing we must not say. A man who was merely a man and said the sort of things Jesus said would not be a great moral teacher. He would either be a lunatic—on the level with the man who says he is a poached egg—or else he would be the Devil of Hell. You must make your choice. Either this man was, and is, the Son of God, or else a madman or something worse. You can shut him up for a fool, you can spit at him and kill him as a demon or you can fall at his feet and call him Lord and God, but let us not come with any patronizing nonsense about his being a great

human teacher. He has not left that open to us. He did not intend to.….Now it seems to me obvious that He was neither a lunatic nor a fiend: and consequently, however strange or terrifying or unlikely it may seem, I have to accept the view that He was and is God.

To me, the choice is clear. My prayer is that the information I've presented will set you on a path that will lead you to the truth, and to the One who waits for you with open arms.

Keith A. Robinson
July, 2016

(Lewis, C.S., *Mere Christianity*, London: Collins, 1952, pp. 54–56. [In all editions, this is Bk. II, Ch. 3, "The Shocking Alternative."])

SUGGESTED RESOURCES

BOOKS

The Case for Christ by Lee Strobel
The Case for Faith by Lee Strobel
The Case for a Creator by Lee Strobel
Evidence That Demands a Verdict by Josh McDowell
World Religions in a Nutshell by Ray Comfort
World Religions and Cults: Counterfeits of Christianity (Volume
    1), by Bodie Hodge and Roger Patterson

WEBSITES

Apologetics Fiction (www.apologeticsfiction.com), the official
    website for Keith A. Robinson.
Apologetics 315 (www.apologetics315.com), a great hub listing
    other apologetics websites, podcasts, and articles.
Probe (www.probe.org), the website for Probe Ministries, full of
    great articles and materials.
Lee Strobel (www.leestrobel.com), the official website for Lee
    Strobel; also full of great videos, articles, etc.
Answers in Genesis (www.answersingenesis.org): Although
    this website has mostly articles that deal with creation and

evolution, there are many other great videos and articles available on a variety of topics regarding Christianity.

Living Waters (www.livingwaters.com), the website for Ray Comfort and Kirk Cameron's ministry.

OTHER BOOKS BY KEITH A. ROBINSON

THE ORIGINS TRILOGY

Book 1: *Logic's End* – In 2034, Rebecca Evans travels to a distant planet searching for life. But when she arrives, she finds a world where survival of the fittest is played out to its logical end. Forced to accept help from mutated animal-like creatures, Rebecca struggles to get off the planet, and soon begins to question everything she once believed about evolution.

Book 2: *Pyramid of the Ancients* – Four years after *Logic's End*, Rebecca's husband, Jeffrey, discovers a mysterious two-story pyramid buried in the sands of Iraq, which turns out to be a machine. When activated, it takes Rebecca, Jeffrey, and a team of scientists backward into time on a journey that challenges their theories about the history of the earth.

Book 3: Escaping the Cataclysm – Picking up where *Pyramid* leaves off, the team fights against all odds to escape from the time just before Noah's flood and return to the future.

ABOUT KEITH A. ROBINSON

AUTHOR OF *THE ORIGINS TRILOGY* AND *THE TARTARUS CHRONICLES*

Keith Robinson has dedicated his life to teaching others how to defend the Christian faith. Since the release of *Logic's End*, his first novel, he has been a featured speaker at Christian music festivals, homeschool conventions, apologetics seminars, and churches, as well as appearing as a guest on numerous radio shows.

Since completing his Origins Trilogy, Mr. Robinson has been working on *The Tartarus Chronicles*, a new series of action/adventure novels dealing with the topic of world religions and worldviews.

When not writing or speaking, Mr. Robinson is the full-time public school orchestra director at the Kenosha School of Technology Enhanced Curriculum, and he is a professional freelance violist and violinist in the Southeastern Wisconsin/Northeastern Illinois area. He currently resides in Kenosha, Wisconsin, with his wife, Stephanie, their five children, and a Rottweiler named Thor.